"What are we going to use for diapers?"

"I know," Jake said suddenly. He reached for his belt buckle.

At Mariel's shocked look, he said, "Don't worry. I'm taking off my long johns. But I'm wearing briefs underneath."

She held the baby to her breasts and turned her head, trying to ignore the sounds of his undressing. Out of the corners of her eyes, she could see him clearly by the light of the fire, clad only in turtleneck and briefs.

He caught her staring at him and seemed to draw himself to his full height, a desirable male exhibiting himself more fully to a female who was clearly admiring.

With a grin, he said, "I thought you weren't planning to look."

Dear Reader,

Perhaps we most feel the magic of Christmas when we kiss that special person under the mistletoe. Or maybe we feel it during a midnight service on Christmas Eve, when the faces of those we love glow with reflected candlelight. Or possibly it's when our children, their smiles outshining the Christmas-tree lights, find their hearts' desires tied up in red tissue paper on Christmas morning.

Who can doubt Christmas magic when so many of us make time during these short days of winter to help those less fortunate than ourselves? Or when we answer the phone on Christmas Day and hear the voice of a dear friend calling to wish us happy holidays from thousands of miles away? Or when we awake on Christmas morning to a fresh snowfall and find a world made sparkly and new?

Christmas is special. It is a time for wassail and wreaths and mistletoe. It is a time for cherishing friends and family and home.

Wherever you find your special magic this holiday season, I hope it brings you love. And joy. And peace.

With best wishes for a merry, magical Christmas,

Pamela

Pamela Browning

PAMELA BROWNING

MERRY CHRISTMAS, BABY

Harlequin Books

TORONTO • NEW YORK • LONDON
AMSTERDAM • PARIS • SYDNEY • HAMBURG
STOCKHOLM • ATHENS • TOKYO • MILAN
MADRID • WARSAW • BUDAPEST • AUCKLAND

ISBN 0-373-16516-1

MERRY CHRISTMAS, BABY

Chapter One

Mariel Evans cruised her car smoothly down the ramp from the interstate highway and peered anxiously at her surroundings.

There was no gas station in sight on this December afternoon two days before Christmas. And an ice storm was approaching from the west, with sleet and freezing rain already falling steadily.

A glance at the gauge reminded Mariel that the gas tank was almost empty, and she knew it would be foolish to attempt to reach the next exit.

Then she saw it—a rusty sign tacked to a tree.

GAS—EATS 2 MI, the lettering said. An arrow pointed left.

In this mountainous part of northern Virginia, Mariel's faithful little Chevy could probably coast the two miles. It might have to.

The rain was falling harder now, and the swish of the car's windshield wipers barely kept up with it. The crackling voice of the radio announcer informed her that this was the worst ice storm to hit the state in thirty years.

This news was hardly reassuring, but the farther north she traveled, the likelier she was to outrun the storm. Now, watching anxiously for the promised GAS—EATS, Mariel proceeded with extreme caution. When the bright red sign of the Magic Minimart came into view, she breathed a grateful sigh of relief, but only until she realized that she'd have to pump her own gas.

Christmas was Mariel's favorite season of the year. Her heart was full of peace and goodwill. So why should she begrudge the Magic Minimart's employees their party?

Through the wide plate-glass window, she saw them inside, whooping it up. The cashier was draped over the cash register, flirting with a guy wearing a Santa hat. A boom box parumpa-pum-pummed "The Little Drummer Boy" so loudly that the music vibrated the concrete beneath Mariel's feet. A man on a ladder was decking the men's room sign with boughs of holly.

And Mariel's fingers were so numb that she couldn't force the gas nozzle to separate from the pump.

"Looks like you could use some help," said a cheerful voice at her elbow. She wheeled around, sure that only a moment ago there had been no one near.

The guy inside wearing the Santa Claus cap couldn't hold a Christmas candle to this roly-poly little man, whose bright blue eyes twinkled up at her over a bushy white beard and a short red jacket.

Before Mariel could say "Jolly old Saint Nicholas," the man had pried her fingers from the handle of the gas pump and was expertly uncapping her gas tank.

"Why, thank you," Mariel said, smiling at him. To look at him made her heart feel happy, as if the sun were shining. Which was ridiculous, considering the fact that rain was dripping down her neck.

"Terrible weather we're having," said the little man.

"I know. And I have to drive all the way to Pittsburgh. I couldn't find a motel room. I guess you'd say there was no room at the inn," she said, trying to make a joke of it.

The little man's eyes snapped with a kind of droll wit. "That happens." He stopped pumping gas and screwed the cap on the tank.

"This is really nice of you," Mariel said. But she couldn't figure out if he worked here. "Do I pay you, or do I go inside?"

"No charge."

"But—"

"It's Christmas," he said with a sage shrug of his shoulders. "Got to get into the spirit of things, you know."

"Well, thanks. And—and merry Christmas." Mariel prepared to get into the car.

"You know, I could tell you a shortcut back to the interstate," the man offered thoughtfully. His beard was rimed with ice.

"Could you? Oh, that would be wonderful!" said Mariel.

"Instead of going back the way you came, take this road in the other direction. When you get to the blinker, turn left, then left again."

"Left, then left again," Mariel repeated.

"It'll be a lot better for you," he said solemnly.

"Thank you. You've been very kind."

"Merry Christmas. And I hope you have a happy New Year, too," he said. He stepped back from the car, and Mariel drove away from the station. When she glanced into her rearview mirror before pulling onto the highway, she expected to see him. But no one was there.

Well. Now to get on with her journey. Even though all that was waiting for her in Pittsburgh was an empty apartment and friends with busy holiday agendas, she couldn't wait to get there. She'd bake cookies for the neighbors, she'd go out and cut lots of pungent evergreen branches to drape across the mantel, and she'd invite the neighborhood kids in for a story hour.

Christmas was always such a magical time. Mariel loved the season and the celebration of it; she looked forward to it all year. If she were granted a pocketful of magic wishes right now, she'd wish for a miracle—that she were already home. She'd wish that it wasn't raining so hard that she could see no more than three feet in front of her car. And she'd wish she could remember if that funny little man had told her how far it was to the blinker. She'd driven miles—or so it seemed—and she hadn't seen a blinker yet.

JAKE TRAVIS DECIDED to take a shortcut back to Tellurian.

He was about ten miles from the new house where he'd been putting the final touches on the finish carpentry so that the owners could move in on the day before Christmas. It was a big deal to them—they wanted to be in their own place for the holidays.

So he'd worked long and hard, and this storm had caught him by surprise. If he'd known it was coming, he would have left for home hours ago.

Old Blue, his aged pickup truck, hugged the curve in the road as he cautiously accelerated for increased traction. If he didn't have to slam on the brakes, Old Blue would do just fine.

Normally Jake took good care of things. That included Old Blue, the only constant in his life. Jake bought beat-up houses and refurbished them, selling them for a pretty penny, moving on when he had to. He didn't even keep a cat.

A truck with four-wheel drive would be nice in this kind of weather. Hell, *brakes* would be nice. Why hadn't he had these lousy brakes fixed last week, when he'd noticed the problem? It was those people, that family. He'd busted his buns so that they could be in their house for Christmas, and now look at him—paying the price for his generosity.

Bah, humbug, he said to himself, thinking that this road didn't look like the shortcut. He couldn't recall the shortcut tunneling through the midst of the forest; nor could he remember its being so dark. Driving this road was like navigating the inside of a cow, and he hadn't passed a house or another car since he turned off the highway.

He pumped cautiously on the brakes, which did little good. He'd have to be careful, the way ice was building up on the asphalt road. Mist swirled ahead of him, graying the landscape, which was probably just as well. The countryside wasn't much to look at.

What I wouldn't give for a cup of hot coffee, he was thinking when a rabbit darted in front of his wheels and he slammed on the—Oh, no! No brakes!

BACK TO THAT pocketful of wishes, Mariel was thinking as she noticed with some trepidation that the trees seemed to be closing over the road.

If she were granted three wishes right *now,* she'd wish for snow that lay "roundabout, deep and crisp and even," as in the carol "Good King Wenceslas." And she'd like a cup of hot spiced cider. *And someone special to share it with,* she thought. *Let's not forget that.*

At the age of thirty, she'd begun to think that her special someone didn't exist. Or if he did, she'd never find him. Her standards, according to her friends, were impossibly high.

Blap, blap, went her windshield wipers, and then they stalled for a moment. They started again in time for her to see that this road merged with another up ahead, but it was not soon enough for her to avoid the streak of blue hurtling out of the fog.

Mariel heard a sickening crunch of metal. Her car skidded out of control toward the ditch, long gray tree branches stabbing at the glass of the windshield, and she clung to the steering wheel for dear life until the car stopped spinning.

Silence. Then she was aware of rain drumming on the metal roof, and a rhythmic roar in her ears that she knew must be her own blood pulsing in her veins.

She opened her eyes, taking stock. She was shaken, but she could move all her fingers and all her toes. The car was resting against a couple of trees, the two right wheels suspended over the ditch. She unfastened her seat belt and then felt as if her heart had stopped. It wasn't a ditch. It was a deep ravine. Treetops were barely visible below.

Panic sluiced over her, freezing her into inaction. In that moment, she knew sheer terror, knew it intimately. In her mind's eye, she could see her car careening into nothingness and taking her with it. In that moment, she felt utterly alone.

"Don't move!" shouted the man who appeared at her window, and she stared at him wildly, wondering if he was an apparition or—as unlikely as it seemed—a real person.

Whatever he was, he looked very worried. Mariel peered up at him on a slant, taking in high, craggy cheekbones and a squared-off chin, a prominent brow and a lone wet strand of dark hair escaping his stocking cap. The man's brown eyes were intriguingly flecked with amber, and they flickered with concern. Despite the cold and damp, Mariel felt a rush of heat. This man was gorgeous. And—no doubt about it now—he was real.

"Are you hurt?" he demanded.

"I don't think so," Mariel said, tentatively finding her voice.

"Keep still. I'm going to stand back now and take a look at this situation."

He scrambled across a boulder and studied the car. Carefully, and very, very slowly, Mariel clasped her seat belt around her again. The way her car was suspended half in space, she wouldn't be surprised if it lurched suddenly.

Through the rain, Mariel saw that the man was big and broad-shouldered. He wore a red-and-black plaid lumberjack jacket, and he appeared to be fit and strong. Below the jacket, well-worn jeans hugged his calves. He studied the position of the car intently, his brow furrowed in concentration. She tried to breathe deeply in order to calm herself, but without success. Her breath came in shallow little bursts, somehow inhibited by the sheer masculinity of this man who wanted to help her.

The stranger hurried toward her. She started to roll down the window, but he said sharply, "Don't do that!"

She must have looked startled, because his expression softened.

"I can get you out of here. But we don't want to take any chances, and the way your car is leaning against those trees, the slightest movement this way or that could change things real fast. Understand?"

She nodded mutely.

He loped off into the fog, and Mariel thought suddenly that she might never see him again.

The windows began to mist, and she resisted the impulse to wipe them clear with her hand. *If I had three wishes,* she started to think, but before she could clarify them, her rescuer was back with a tool kit and a long length of chain.

"I'll have you out of there in a few minutes," he promised. She only looked at him. Every time she allowed herself to glance toward the ravine, her stomach rolled over.

The man ducked beneath the car. She heard and felt the rasp of the chain against metal, and then he reappeared and wrapped the other end securely around a couple of immense trees.

He yanked at the end of the chain to test it. "I think that'll hold it," he said, coming around to her window again. He bent over and looked at her, and under the influence of his calm gaze she felt her shoulders relax.

"I tied the chain around the chassis in a couple of places. If the car falls, it can't go far," he said.

"What do you want me to do?" It occurred to her that this stranger could be some kind of nut, but he *was* trying to save her life.

He considered, gazing off into the treetops below for a long moment. "I'm going to see if I can get your door open. The metal's kind of crumpled, so it may not work," he said.

Sure enough, it didn't.

"Want me to try opening it from the inside?" she asked, wanting to show him that she was cooperating. It seemed important to her that he know that he could count on her.

"Go ahead."

She tried. The door wouldn't budge.

"I'll roll down the window, and you can reach in and try," she said.

The man nodded. Slowly she cranked the handle, and the window eased down. Fog floated into the car; the mist felt cool against her hot cheeks. The man reached in and exerted a steady pressure on the door handle. His hand was square, and his fingers were long.

"Excuse me for a minute. I've got to go get a tool out of my truck," the man said. He strode away, the red and black of his jacket weaving through the forest until he disappeared altogether.

Mariel almost released her seat belt again, then decided against it. The stranger seemed to be in complete control. She'd be better off following his directions, since he seemed to know what he was doing.

When he returned, he was carrying a tire iron. Again Mariel worried. There were a number of things you could do with a tire iron, and one of them was hitting somebody over the head. Though if that was what he had in mind, he was going to a lot of trouble to do it.

"You can take off the seat belt now," he said briskly. "Then I'm going to pry at the door. Be ready to move fast if you have to."

Mariel braced herself. He pried. Nothing happened to the door, but the car settled against its supporting trees with a tired wheeze. The treetops in the ravine spun sickeningly, and Mariel thought of her three wishes.

"A parachute. A hot-air balloon. And a can opener," she said.

"What?" asked the man.

"Just...um, making a few wishes," she said, feeling foolish.

His look was scornful. "If you're crazy enough to think that wishes will work, how about wishing for the rain to let up?"

She frowned. Where did he get off, calling her crazy? Nevertheless, she canceled the hot-air balloon anyway, mentally adding "no rain" to her wish list.

"You'd think they'd make these car doors with pop-off hinges or something," he said.

"I doubt that designers of cars think about all the things that can happen," Mariel said reasonably.

"They should," he said with a grunt. "They should sit around and brainstorm all the worst things that could go wrong. They should say, 'What if one of our cars is dangling over a ravine with a woman inside?' All kinds of things can happen, you know. Driving is unpredictable."

"Life is unpredictable. Nobody makes *life* with pop-off hinges, either," Mariel returned.

"Yeah, well, you were talking about wishes. You sounded as if you believed wishing might work."

"Sometimes it does. I do believe in magic," Mariel said defensively.

He paused and studied her for a moment. "Weird," was all he said before inserting the tip of the tire iron in a new place between car door and frame.

"There *are* miracles," Mariel said.

"That so?" he asked, as if he weren't really paying attention. Mariel heard metal bending, but the door still didn't open.

"What do you call, um . . . well, for instance, spring-time? When everything is fresh and new again, and flowers bloom, and grass grows, and—"

He spared her a brief look of disdain. "I'd call springtime a welcome relief at this point," he said succinctly.

Mariel sat back, thinking that what she had here was a realist, not a dreamer. In these circumstances, she couldn't say that was all bad.

"There!" he said, jabbing the tire iron one last time. Something bent and snapped, and he peeled the door back. Mariel, seeing an opportunity, started to scramble out of the car.

"Stop!" he yelled, grabbing at her wrist and missing it.

The car rolled slightly forward, and Mariel screamed. He caught her wrist this time, and with a tremendous surge of strength he hauled her out of her seat.

She staggered against him, and he held her in his arms. The wool of his jacket was soft against her cheek, and the length of his body against hers felt warm and reassuring. She clung to him, aware of firm muscles beneath his jacket and his gaze riveted on her face.

"Whoa," he said. "That was some predicament." For the first time, she was aware of his unmistakably southern drawl. It felt gentle on her ears.

"It was close," she agreed shakily, looking back over her shoulder. Her poor little Chevy hung over the edge of the world, its left side sideswiped, one of its headlights dangling from the socket.

"You really are all right?" he asked, and she focused her eyes to see that his face was filled with concern.

"I'm okay. Didn't you see that yield sign where the roads met?"

"I—Well, it was those fool brakes. Should have had them fixed, but I neglected it."

Mariel rolled her eyes in exasperation. "You mean I was in that fix because you were too lazy to take your truck to the garage?" she asked incredulously.

"I had to finish the carpentry in a house where I was working so the owners could move in before Christmas," he said defensively.

"Great," Mariel said through gritted teeth. "Talk about the designers of cars not thinking about all the things that could happen. Didn't it occur to you that brakes are important? That they need to be in proper working order?"

"I didn't think—" he began.

"Obviously," Mariel said, to cut him off.

His jaw was set in a grim line. "I'm glad you're not hurt. I'd never forgive myself if you were," he said, which redeemed him somewhat in Mariel's eyes.

"I don't know your name," she said.

"Jake. Jake Travis. And yours?"

"Mariel Evans," she replied.

"What a way to meet," he said glumly.

"What do we do now? I didn't see any houses, or a place where we could phone for help, did you?" she asked. The fog amplified her voice, and her words echoed back at her.

"No phones, I'm afraid. I must have taken a wrong turn, but how did *you* end up way out here?" He was eyeing her Pennsylvania license plate.

"I followed the directions of a man who helped me at a gas station near the interstate," she said. "I must have gotten them wrong. I have no idea where we are."

"Neither do I, and I live twenty miles away. Well, let's see if Old Blue will crank up." He grasped her elbow and started to steer her past the dank, dripping trees toward the patch of blue in the mist.

"Wait," she said, holding back. "I'd better get my purse out of the car."

"Oh, no, you don't. I don't trust the way it's leaning."

"I can reach in and grab it," she said evenly. She marched toward the car, but he was past her in a minute, opening the damaged door and peering inside.

"I'll do it."

"You're too heavy. If you lean your weight on the car, it's going to move," Mariel argued.

"Who said anything about leaning? Anyway, I tied the frame of the car to the tree as tightly as I could."

"The car moved when I got out," Mariel reminded him.

He heaved an impatient sigh. "All right. I'll hold your hand while you lean in. Don't touch the car, just grab the purse."

"And my tote bag from in front of the passenger seat."

"Okay, okay. Just get on with it," he said. "Hold on to me." He extended his hand.

Reluctantly she reached toward him.

"No, not that way," he said. "You hold my wrist, I'll hold yours. It'll be stronger." He demonstrated, and as her hand held tight to his wrist, she felt the sinews contracting. He seemed as strong as he looked.

As soon as they had a secure grip on each other, Mariel leaned gingerly into the car. Already her little Chevy, which had seen her through a marriage, a divorce and two cross-country trips, seemed alien, different, not part of her anymore. She picked up the purse and stuffed it into the tote bag, and Jake hauled her up and out of the car.

He didn't let go of her wrist right away. His hand was warm, and she felt her pulse beating against his palm. Flustered, she pulled her hand away.

"Let's go get in my truck," he said, so she slung the tote bag on her shoulder and followed him.

Jake's truck wasn't much newer than her own car, but it seemed well maintained. He got in and leaned over the seat to open the door on the passenger side. Mariel climbed in, giving Jake points for the cleanliness and neatness of the cab.

He noticed that she was shivering. "As soon as the engine is warm, I'll turn the heater on full blast," he promised. She nodded. Her relief and subsequent anger with Jake had evaporated, leaving her feeling perilously close to tears. She shoved her hands deep in the pockets of her coat and stared out the window.

Icicles were beginning to form on drooping tree limbs, and Mariel leaned her aching head against the cool window glass. Idly she noticed pale, parasitic clumps of waxy green leaves growing in the treetops, and recognized them as mistletoe. *How appropriate to the Christmas season,* she thought. She had never seen mistletoe growing in the wild before. She'd always been partial to the contrast of the ivory berries against the paler oval leaves. She usually used it liberally in her holiday decorating, and not only for its effect on her love life. She simply liked the way it looked.

But for now, holiday decor was the last thing she wanted to think about. She felt stiff and sore all over, and her head ached. A warm bed with an electric blanket turned all the way to "bake" would feel wonderful at this point.

The truck engine turned over but wouldn't start.

Jake jiggled the ignition key and tried again. Nothing.

"The battery's new," Jake said. He got out and raised the hood, disappearing under it for so long that Mariel began to suspect that the problem was major. When he climbed back in beside her, he looked worried. And when he tried to start the motor again, the battery only clicked a few times and died.

"That's it," he said, a grim tone to his voice. "We won't be going anywhere in Old Blue."

"This," Mariel said wearily, "is a nightmare."

"You said it," Jake answered.

They listened to the rain falling for a while, and then Jake said abruptly, "We can't stay here. It's going to get colder tonight. I think we should strike out and try to find a house. Otherwise..." His words trailed off, and Mariel understood that he considered it dangerous to stay in the truck.

For the first time, she realized their peril. They were lost in the woods, their vehicles out of commission, with the worst ice storm in thirty years roaring out of the west. Without a warm place to stay, they could freeze to death.

Jake regarded her across the wide expanse of vinyl seat. "I passed no place fit for human habitation on the road I traveled, and there's nothing where you came from, either. If we continue the way we were headed, I think we'll come to civilization. There's a major highway in that direction," he said.

"The interstate?" Mariel asked hopefully.

"I think the interstate is the other way. The road I'm thinking of is the highway into the town where I live."

Mariel sighed. "I'm game. I can't see sitting here and waiting for help to come along, when it may not."

"Good," Jake said, smiling at her. He had a nice smile; his teeth were very white. One bicuspid lapped slightly over the adjoining tooth, which only made the smile more interesting. Mariel wished he'd take off his cap so that she could see his hair.

When Jake hopped out of the truck cab, Mariel did, too. "What are you doing?" she asked when he climbed up over the open tailgate onto the bed of the truck and opened a metal box.

"Getting a few tools."

"For what?" she asked. She had to crane her neck to look at him.

"I was a Boy Scout once. We believe in being prepared," he told her, jumping down.

Mariel couldn't resist smiling at him. She wondered how old he was. Thirty-two? Thirty-three? It was impossible to tell, but then he probably couldn't tell much about her, either. She was wrapped in her tan, all-weather coat with the wool lining, her hair tucked under the collar, a red scarf wound up to her ears.

Now she flipped a corner of the scarf over her hair to protect it from the rain.

"Ready?" Jake asked. He shrugged into a small backpack and tugged at the straps until it fitted comfortably over his jacket.

Mariel nodded. With a last look at the truck, which, even though inoperative, represented a dry place to shelter from the weather, she resolutely faced the road. Whatever her fortunes, she had cast them with this stranger.

There was no use looking back. Anyway, it was too much trouble. Her neck hurt.

With the freezing rain stinging her face, and wearing boots that were designed for style rather than tramping along an ice-slicked road, Mariel followed Jake into the eddying mist.

Chapter Two

The road beneath their feet was so icy that it was difficult to keep a firm footing, and Jake kept a covert eye on his companion. She marched up and down the hills like a trooper, thank goodness, and he had the feeling that she was determined not to slow him down.

"So, Mariel, what brings you to this part of the country?"

"My job," she said. "I'm a folklorist for a museum in Pittsburgh, and they sent me to a conference in Roanoke. I was on my way home—I thought."

A glance down at her revealed that her blue eyes were dancing with a kind of rueful humor. He was glad to see it; he had a feeling that she'd need it before this day was over. He didn't look away immediately, because he was suddenly fascinated with her face. He hadn't realized before what a good-looking woman she was.

"What do you do?" she asked.

"I'm a carpenter by trade. Thus the tools," he said, gesturing over his shoulder at the small pack he wore. In it were things he hoped they wouldn't need—matches, leftovers from his lunch, a flashlight, hatchet, hammer, rope, and a Swiss army knife. He didn't want to talk about himself, though. He'd rather learn more about her.

"Tell me what a folklorist does," he said, trying to sound interested.

"I collect legends and catalog them," she said easily.

"How'd you get a job like that?"

"Oh, I have a master's degree in history, and I wrote my thesis on the origins of legends."

"Sounds boring. I guess that's why I never went to college."

She smiled. "It's not boring to me. I'm gathering stories to show how Christmas legends developed. You'd be surprised how many of them evolved similarly in different countries."

"Such as what? And where?"

"Such as gift-givers in all sorts of cultures. We're familiar with the real Saint Nicholas, who was probably a bishop in Asia Minor in the fourth century and is the basis for our Santa Claus. And there was the ancient Roman hag, Befana, who searched the world, leaving candy for good children, stones for the bad. And there was Knecht Ruprecht, a straw-clad German spirit who gave gifts to good children—"

"Sounds pagan to me," Jake said mildly, interrupting her.

Mariel turned wide eyes upon him. "Many of our customs had pagan origins. Take Christmas customs, for instance. People in primitive times lived very close to nature, you see, and they were quite aware of the shortest day of the year, which is December twenty-second. They celebrated when the days started to grow longer, and so we have celebrations of winter cropping up in every culture."

Jake hunched his shoulders against the rain, which was turning to sleet. "The middle of the winter's not much to celebrate, in my opinion," he muttered.

"Oh, but the celebration was to banish the winter doldrums, you see. To cheer everyone up," she said.

A curly blond tendril had escaped the scarf protecting her head, and Jake had the ridiculous urge to reach out and push it back.

"You and I ought to be celebrating, I guess," he said. "We could certainly banish *these* winter doldrums, and that's a fact." His words evaporated into a vapor trail; the air temperature was dropping.

She was silent while they walked another half mile or so. He thought maybe he had offended her, but in his opinion, the whole conversation was silly. Its only merit was that it helped him to know her better.

"I wonder how far we've come." He turned around and walked backward a few steps. The road behind them was shrouded in mist, and a tree limb fell suddenly, startling both of them.

"Strange that no one lives near here," Mariel said, her voice echoing eerily in the surrounding forest.

"I'm sure we'll come upon a house soon," Jake said, with more bravado than he felt. Mariel was still walking pluckily along beside him, but her step seemed less springy, and a tense line bisected her forehead. The veins beneath the skin at her temple were blue; her skin was milky white.

"This isn't supposed to happen at Christmas," she said. "We should be home among our friends and family, our cheeks nice and rosy, comfy-cozy, roasting chestnuts on an open fire."

"Right, but Jack Frost is nipping at my nose, and we'd better not slow down, or we're going to turn into snowmen right here and now."

She glanced at him sideways. "Oh, but you have to keep the Christmas spirit, no matter what happens. That's the whole idea."

"I've never cared much for Christmas," he said tightly. "All that family stuff—well, I never experienced it. As far as I'm concerned, this holiday is one where I get a few days off work, for which, since I'm self-employed, I don't get paid. If I'm lucky, on Christmas Day someone will take pity on me and invite me over for turkey dinner. Then the men of the family and I will watch a football game. Afterward I'll go home to an empty house."

Mariel seemed taken aback. "You're not married?" she asked.

"No. And I've never had any family. I grew up in a series of foster homes. For Christmas I usually got a few pairs of socks and some underwear. There was no Santa Claus for me—ever."

"No Santa? Why that's—that's..."

"That's the breaks of the game," he finished for her. "Do you think you could walk a bit faster? It's getting late, which means it's going to be dark soon."

"You set the pace. I'll keep up," she said stoically, and so he sped up. Walking slightly ahead of her, he was able to hide the expression on his face, which he was sure wasn't pleasant.

He just didn't like thinking about Santa Claus, that was all. The whole idea of a jolly little man who lavished gifts on people who already had everything they needed made him angry. If there really *were* a Santa Claus, he'd give things to people who needed them. The whole Christmas thing was enough to make him Santa Clauseated, which rhymed with nauseated, which was a pretty bad joke, and he already knew there was no point in saying it to Mariel.

THEY HAD BEEN WALKING for about an hour when Mariel spied something that looked like a roof through the trees. At first she couldn't believe her eyes. She'd begun to think they were walking along the most deserted road on earth.

"A house! Over there!" she exclaimed, clutching Jake's arm.

He clapped his hand over hers and broke into a smile. "I knew someone must live along here. Careful, don't trip in that pothole," he said, taking her gloved hand in his and pulling her along. Above them, bare, icy branches seemed to lock arms overhead, creaking and complaining with the rising wind.

A path, almost overgrown with bushes, led to the little house. Such a funny little house, Mariel thought, and she didn't see any windows or any lights.

Jake stopped so suddenly that she almost ran into him. "It's just an old hunter's blind, not a house at all," he said. "Look, the roof is crumbling."

"Oh," Mariel said on a soft sigh of disappointment.

They made their way around to the hidden side of the structure. "Why, it's nothing but a lean-to," Mariel said.

Jake kicked at a few loose boards. "There's no point in staying. This place wouldn't be any better shelter than my truck. Speaking of which, maybe we shouldn't have left."

"I don't know," said Mariel. "I'm cold and hungry and I ache all over. I wish somebody would come along and give us a lift back to the Magic Minimart where all my problems started, and—''

Jake interrupted her. ''No more of your wishes. So far you're batting zero.''

They both heard the cry at the same time.

''What's that?'' Jake asked in alarm.

''It sounds like a baby crying.''

''A baby? Here? No, it could be an animal, or maybe a bird, but a baby? No way,'' Jake said, as though there could be no doubt. ''Come on, we'd better get out of here. This place gives me the creeps.'' He walked away, his hands deep in his pockets, his boots tramping down the wet brown leaves. The set of his shoulders was resolute, and he didn't look back.

Mariel readjusted the scarf over her hair and groped in her pocket for a tissue. She was stuffing it back into her pocket when she heard the cry again. Not the strong, full-bodied cry of an older child, but the high, thin wail of a small baby.

She looked toward Jake, whose bright jacket was barely visible through the wet tree trunks. She almost followed him. She certainly didn't want to lose him, and she didn't want him to think that she was slowing down. But how could she ignore a baby's cry?

''Mariel! Hurry up!'' he called.

Impulsively Mariel pushed aside a rotting, rain-soaked board and entered the hut. It took her eyes a moment to adjust to the gloom, but when they did, she was astonished to see, lying on a bed of dry leaves and wrapped in a sturdy pink blanket, a tiny infant.

The baby's face was red and screwed up into a furious wail. Small fists flailed the air, and beneath the blanket little feet kicked.

"Jake!" Mariel called, falling to her knees and gathering the child into her arms. The baby stopped crying at once and stared, openmouthed, at Mariel.

She heard Jake crashing through the underbrush. He appeared at the entrance to the hut, his eyes wild. "What's the matter?"

For an answer, Mariel slowly rose to her feet and turned so that he could see the child. His eyes widened.

"It *was* a baby!" he said in a strangled voice.

The air between them seemed very heavy.

Jake's cap had fallen off, and he ran his fingers through his hair. It was dark brown and wavy, crisp with the cold, and it sprang up under his fingers as if it had a life of its own.

"I'll be damned," he said. He was regarding the baby with distaste.

"We can't leave it here," Mariel said.

"Of course not," he said. "How did it get here in the first place, that's what I'd like to know." Jake's sweeping gaze took in the dilapidated shelter, icicles forming where water dripped from the roof. His eyes met Mariel's. He looked angry and disgusted.

"Does it matter how she got here?" Mariel asked. She cradled the baby protectively in her arms and pressed her cheek to the top of the infant's head. Despite Jake's dismay, Mariel felt a thrill of excitement. She parted the blanket and counted ten fingers and ten toes. The baby was a girl, and Mariel thought she might be a month old. She wore a pink flannel nightgown and a dry cloth diaper. She had a curl of pale yellow fuzz atop her head, and she was beautiful.

The baby made little mewling noises, not unlike those of a newborn kitten. Mariel's heart turned over when she realized that she must be hungry.

"Where are her parents?" Jake asked with barely controlled anger. He stomped out of the hut and stared into the woods. Mariel followed, the baby in her arms. They saw no sign of life other than themselves, only wet tree trunks half hidden in fog.

"Hello?" Jake called experimentally, hands cupped to his mouth. The word danced around them in echoes, but there was no answer.

"Is anyone there?" Jake shouted, but the forest only cried, "There . . . there . . . there," until the sound died.

"We can't leave this baby," Mariel said again.

Jake threw his head back in exasperation, staring up at the imprisoning branches as if hoping to find an answer. When, after a long moment, he looked back at Mariel, his eyes were grim.

"With the light fading, we can't let the baby slow our progress," he said, in a tone that struggled to be matter-of-fact.

"Of course not."

"And she's an added responsibility. I don't know anything about babies. Do you?"

Mariel bit her lip and gazed down into the chubby little face.

"Well, do you?" he demanded.

"Not a thing," she admitted.

"How are we going to take care of her?"

"We'll have to manage," she said, lifting her chin. "We can do it. We have no choice. We have to get her someplace warm and feed her and—and everything," Mariel said.

"What kind of person would leave a child out in this weather? I'd like to get my hands on him," Jake said. He pulled his cap securely down over his forehead. "I'd better carry her."

"But I—"

"Your feet were slipping and sliding on the ice, I noticed. I'm wearing work boots with a tread. It's a matter of safety."

"I am perfectly capable—" Mariel began.

"Mariel," Jake said gruffly, "give her to me. You're wasting time."

Stung by Jake's tone, Mariel reluctantly handed the baby to him. The child settled against Jake's chest as if she felt perfectly comfortable there, the pink blanket incongruous against his bold plaid jacket. Mariel solicitously reached over and pulled a fold of the blanket over the baby's face to protect her from the sleet.

"Ready?" Jake said. He held the bundle awkwardly, and his face was stony, unreadable.

Mariel nodded silently, her heart in her throat. She wasn't responsible for the baby's being there, but Jake seemed to be angry with her. This situation was hard enough without having to take that kind of flak.

Making her way at a slower pace, Mariel followed Jake back through the woods to the road. Water dripped from bare branches; patches of dense fog filled the hollows. It wouldn't be long before it was completely dark. The thought of being stranded in these woods in the cold and the dark with sleet falling all around made her shiver.

If she talked, maybe she could jolt Jake into a better mood. If she kept talking, maybe she wouldn't think about the danger.

"Tell me about the town where you live," Mariel said to Jake, struggling to keep her teeth from chattering.

"Why?" His expression was uncompromising, and it only softened slightly when he glanced at Mariel. The baby was snuggled in his arms and wasn't making a peep.

"Because I want to know about it," she said.

"Now? While we're walking along in this sleet? Just after we find a baby in the woods?" he asked incredulously.

"I just want to talk," she said through gritted teeth. When he saw the dark look on her face—the first sign of negativity since they'd started out—he seemed to think better about resisting conversation and began to talk.

His voice was deep and reassuring as they walked through the darkening woods, the sleet cold and wet against their faces.

"Tellurian," Jake said, "is a picture-book town folded into a valley in these mountains, the Shenandoahs. I live on a tree-shaded street in a big, rambling house with old-fashioned plumbing and beautiful hardwood floors and a kitchen with oak cabinets that I built myself," he said, walking briskly to set their pace.

"Go on," she said, keeping her eyes on the road. Ahead was another hill, and she dreaded the climb.

"I buy houses and fix them up, then I sell them. I like working with wood, shaping a board into something beautiful. I like the clean smell of the wood, as well as the feel of it, and I like the way the people who buy my houses admire my handiwork."

"I can't believe you'd put so much of yourself into a house and then sell it," Mariel said breathlessly. They were walking so fast that she was having a hard time pulling enough air into her lungs. Jake was having no difficulty; he swung easily along beside her, planting his feet firmly, the baby hardly any weight at all.

"It's how I make money" was all he said, and she sensed that worldly possessions meant little to him. They walked on, tackling the hill. Mariel was too much out of breath to prod him with more questions. He looked down at her once or twice, and she tried not to let him see how tired she was. Once he slowed his pace slightly, which made walking easier. She sensed he was worried.

I can't let him down, she thought to herself, but at the foot of the hill, she slipped on loose rock and caught his arm, almost knocking him over in the process.

He steadied her, and she peered down at the baby. The infant was quiet, her face barely visible beneath the fold of the blanket. Jake looked at the baby, too, his expression grave.

"Mariel, we're going to have to come to a decision," he said as she leaned against him.

"About what?" she said wearily.

"About which way to go. If it were still only the two of us, I'd say let's forge ahead. But now that we've got this baby, I think we should go back to my truck."

Mariel's head shot up. "We've come all this way and you want to go back where we came from? No way," she said, starting to walk on and expecting him to follow. She hunched her shoulders and concentrated on moving one foot after the other, only to be halted by Jake's imperative tone.

"The truck's a place of shelter from the storm. We don't know how bad it's going to get."

She turned around. He was strong and stolid, standing there with sleet bouncing off his wide shoulders, the baby pressed to his chest. But was he right? *Should* they turn back?

"We already know there's no one for miles in that direction," she said stubbornly. "It's foolish to go back that way."

"We have no idea what lies ahead," he retorted. "Could be better, could be worse. Back there—" he jerked his head to indicate the road along which they'd come "—there's my truck. I vote we go that way."

"A house with heat sounds a lot more inviting. There's bound to be someone in this direction," she argued.

"Don't be stupid!"

"Stupid! May I remind you that we wouldn't be in this fix if you hadn't run me off the road?" Mariel's feet were like blocks of ice now. Her knee and hip joints ached. Never had she felt more miserable.

Darkness was gathering around them, but she saw Jake's brows draw together. Fear stabbed through her. What if he decided to go back to the truck, leaving her to struggle on toward the unknown? Yet she knew in her heart that to turn back would be the wrong thing to do. They already knew there was nothing there, and while the truck might afford a place to shelter from the weather, it wouldn't be warm. She'd rather take her chances on finding a house with welcoming inhabitants up ahead.

Jake was silent for a long time. Too long. Mariel shifted her weight from one foot to the other, wondering if her feet would ever be warm again.

Reluctantly she walked back to where Jake stood and nudged the blanket away from the baby's face. The child looked up at her, blue eyes wide and trusting. In that instant, Mariel felt the full weight of responsibility settle slowly onto her shoulders.

"This baby needs food, Jake. No telling how long it's been since she's eaten," Mariel said, quietly but urgently. She let the fabric fall across the baby's face again, and the child whimpered and nuzzled against Jake's coat.

Jake stared down at the infant in his arms, his brows drawn together. Mariel watched the expressions flit across his face, one after the other—worry, doubt, anguish and, finally, concession.

"All right," he said at last. "You're the one with the college degrees. We'll do it your way."

"What kind of dig is that?" she demanded.

"I didn't mean anything. Let's go." He started walking.

Now that she had convinced him, Mariel felt uncertain. What if they were indeed headed farther into the wilderness? But, no, she instinctively felt that the worst thing they could do would be to turn back.

Quickly, before she could change her mind, she wheeled and caught up with Jake. Anxiously she looked at the bundle that was the baby.

"Do you think she's all right?" she asked.

"She's moving around."

"I guess that's good. I hope wherever we end up, they have clean diapers."

"Dream on," Jake scoffed. After a few minutes he said, "It's getting so dark I can hardly see ahead of us. Can you get the flashlight out of my backpack?" He stopped and turned his back to her, and her fingers struggled with the fastening. He waited patiently, but the baby began to wail.

"You'll have to bend down. I can't reach in," said Mariel.

He bent his knees, and she fumbled for the flashlight. Finally her fingers closed around its handle and she withdrew it and switched it on. The beam bounced around the treetops before settling on the road.

"What else is in that pack of yours?" she asked.

"Some things left over from lunch."

"Anything that would feed a baby?"

"A bit of milk in the thermos."

"We may have to feed her soon." Mariel shone the light on the baby's face as they walked. The infant's eyes were scrunched tightly, and her toothless mouth stretched wider with every wail.

Now that it was dark, Mariel was beginning to feel exhausted. Putting one foot in front of the other was starting to feel like too much of an effort, but she knew she couldn't stop now that she had insisted that they continue in this direction. She wanted to act confident, to make Jake feel as if this had been the right decision.

"I don't see any signs of people," Jake said after they had walked in silence for half an hour or more. The baby had stopped crying after he opened his coat and settled her inside. Mariel supposed Jake was getting tired of carrying the baby, but he hadn't complained.

"Does the road seem narrower to you?" she asked anxiously. She focused the flashlight ahead of them, where the road seemed to become part of the forest.

"I don't know," Jake said. "You look bushed. Want me to carry the flashlight?"

She shook her head. "I'm fine," she said doggedly.

His keen look told her that she didn't look fine, but she was beyond caring. The skin of her face felt raw from the sleet, and the scarf that was supposed to be protecting her hair was soaked through. As a therapeutic exercise, she tried to remember all the warm fireplaces she'd ever known, like the cavernous one at camp where they'd toasted marshmallows on rainy summer nights, and the marble one at the museum, which was used only for patrons' parties in the winter, and the small but cozy fireplace in her apartment, where she would like to be right now.

They walked another hundred yards before the road tapered into a hard-packed dirt track.

"Now what do we do?" Mariel asked in bewilderment.

"We should have gone back to the truck," Jake said tightly.

"We still could," she pointed out.

He glared at her in exasperation. "Look at you. You're barely able to stand up. There's no way you can walk that far."

She stared at him bleakly, knowing it was true.

When he spoke again, Jake's voice was kind. "We'll sit down on that fallen log over there and rest for a few minutes while we figure out what to do."

Mariel's knees buckled just as she reached it. She hoped Jake hadn't noticed.

The infant had been quiet for a long time.

"Is the baby—?" she began fearfully.

"Asleep. I think." Jake opened his coat. The baby's eyes were closed, and her fists were curled against her cheeks like small pink shells.

"Would you hold her while I look around?" Jake asked.

"Of course." Mariel unbuttoned her coat. "I'll hug her inside, next to my sweater."

Carefully Jake transferred the sleeping baby to Mariel's waiting arms, and she drew her inside her coat.

Jake couldn't help feeling tender toward both of them. The baby was so helpless, and Mariel's face was white and strained. He wondered how much longer she'd be able to hold up—and how much longer she would have to.

"You must be freezing," he said, thinking that Mariel was really quite small and more fragile than he had thought.

She nodded. She looked extremely uncomfortable, but not one word of complaint had fallen from her lips throughout this journey, and he had to admire that.

"I won't go far away. Maybe I'd better take the flashlight," he said, picking it up from the log where Mariel had put it.

"I won't be able to see you," Mariel said shakily. Her eyes were like bottomless black pools, and he saw in that moment how scared she really was.

"I'll call to you from time to time," he said, and she nodded. He thought for a moment of leaving the flashlight with her, but what good would that do? He wouldn't be able to see a thing without it.

"Go ahead," Mariel said, wrapping herself around the baby. He saw that Mariel's teeth were chattering, and that she was trying to conceal it from him.

"I hate leaving you here in the pitch dark."

"Just go," she said. "The sooner you leave, the sooner you'll be back."

"Mariel..." He wanted to tell her something to reassure her, but he couldn't think of anything.

"Go," she whispered, her voice barely audible above the sound of the softly falling sleet.

With one last look at both of them—it was a scene that Jake knew would be imprinted on his mind for all time—he turned and forced himself to walk away.

THE FLASHLIGHT made eerie shadows among the trees as Jake walked away from her, and Mariel bent her head down to protect the baby's. She had never felt so completely and awfully alone.

But she wasn't alone. She had the baby.

Jake called to her once or twice, and eventually she saw the beam from the flashlight wavering in another direction. After that, she couldn't see Jake at all.

The baby fussed, and Mariel tried to see her face but couldn't. She felt water dripping off the tip of her nose, and the baby started to cry when it fell in her face. Mariel covered the infant's face with the dry end of her scarf and tried to comfort her, and eventually the cries tapered off into hiccups.

Now that she wasn't moving, Mariel realized the full extent of her exhaustion. She was so tired that she didn't have enough energy to get up off the log, but she thought she should rise and stamp her feet to get her circulation going. She forced herself to stand, surprised at how rubbery her legs felt. Somewhere overhead, a branch cracked under the weight of accumulated ice, crashing through tree limbs and landing on the ground behind her.

Mariel sat down again. She was trembling. There might be bears in these woods, or wolves. She hadn't seen the flashlight beam in a while, and Jake hadn't called. She hoped he was all right.

The cold had numbed her face and her feet and her hands. She thought of her parents, who had gone to Africa six months ago to help with famine-relief efforts. They would be warm. They might be on vacation for the Christmas holiday; her mother had written that they might go on a photo safari. It would be adventurous and different, she'd said.

I'll show you adventurous and different, Mariel thought. She wished she'd joined her parents for Christmas, as they'd asked her to. She wished she'd done anything but wander off the interstate and follow the directions of a bushy-bearded man at a Magic Minimart.

She closed her eyes, willing herself to be in Africa. She saw gazelles leaping across her field of vision, antelopes, and an elephant lumbering toward a river in the distance. The weather was warm, and she was so tired that all she wanted to do was sleep.

Her head fell forward, and it was too much trouble to lift it. She would never open her eyes again, she would sleep here forever, and she would be warm....

"Oh, no, you won't," said a voice in front of her. "Open your eyes, Mariel."

She wanted to speak, but the words wouldn't come out. And her eyes wouldn't open.

"Mariel," said the voice, which was somehow strange and familiar at once.

With great effort, Mariel forced her eyelids apart. In front of her, only a few feet away, stood the little man from the Magic Minimart.

"Who—Who—" she stammered.

"You sound like a frozen owl. Get up! If you don't, you'll freeze to death!" The man's white beard bristled, and his blue eyes were stern.

"But—"

"Hurry up! You have to go find Jake!"

She didn't know what made her follow his instructions; certainly the last time she'd done what he suggested, she'd found herself in a mess. *This* mess. Nevertheless, she struggled to her feet.

"Now get going. No, not *that* way. The other way. That's right. Keep walking through the trees. You'll see the path. Take good care of the baby. She needs you." And with that, the man disappeared.

Mariel blinked her eyes. Had she really seen him, or had he been a dream, like the gazelles and the antelopes?

Her eyes had adjusted to the darkness. She saw a path leading through the trees, a path that she could have sworn hadn't been there before, and she stumbled along it, unsure whether it was the right thing to do. Jake had said to wait for him. And she hadn't heard a sound from him for a long time.

"Jake?" she called, but her voice was so weak that she was sure he wouldn't hear, and she wasn't surprised when he didn't answer.

A MAN ALONE would have a better chance of making it to safety than a man burdened with a woman and a child. Jake couldn't help it; he thought about hoofing it back to his truck, solo. Yet he knew he would never actually do it. Jake Travis was a man who lived up to his responsibilities, and he considered it his fault that Mariel was in this predicament.

He regretted his gruffness toward Mariel back at the hunter's blind, but he'd had to get her moving somehow, and being short with her had seemed like the only way to do it, considering all the commotion she was making over the baby. She sure liked that kid; she didn't seem to mind that the baby might slow them down.

Jake wasn't much for praying, but he found himself doing it. He had to find a place where they could get out of the sleet, a place where they could stay warm. He would probably survive a night in the open, but Mariel might not. No telling what being out in this weather would do to the baby. Jake hadn't mentioned it to Mariel, but the kid hadn't moved much after the last time it cried.

The dirt road continued for fifty yards or so. He veered off the path where a huge fallen tree blocked it, and he changed direction a few times, memorizing his path so that he would be able to return to Mariel and the baby.

The woods were thick here, and icicles had formed on all the branches. When he realized that he had wandered away from the road, he stopped and beamed the flashlight upward. He was shocked to see that he had come up against a sheer rock cliff.

He whistled under his breath. They wouldn't be moving on in this direction, at least. He stood there, taking stock. Perhaps the downed tree he had passed earlier could form the basis for a shelter. They could dig out the ground beneath the trunk and crawl under it.

"Jake?"

He heard Mariel's voice close behind him. "Mariel, how did you find me?" he asked, because he had taken a circuitous route and had had no sense of her following him.

"It wasn't hard."

As Jake swung around, the beam from his light pinned Mariel's pale face in its glare, and he realized that she was barely able to stand. The baby made no sound, and that frightened him.

"You should have stayed where you were," he said, more sharply than he'd intended.

"I was worried. I called, and you didn't answer." She moved toward him, a wraithlike figure in the fog, and he reached out and drew her to him.

"Looks like this is the end of the road," he said, swinging the beam of the flashlight along the face of the cliff.

Mariel didn't answer, and when he looked down at her, he saw that the light had gone out of her eyes.

"Can you take the baby?" she asked shakily. "I want to sit down someplace."

He reached for the bundle, but as he did so, the dimming circle of light from the flashlight picked out a shadow on the face of the cliff.

"Wait," he said to Mariel, sprinting past her. He scraped his knuckles on the rock as he pulled away brambles. He discovered a waist-high hollow in the wet rock, and when he shone the light inside, the hollow expanded into a small cave. The remains of a camp fire were scattered across the sandy floor.

"Hey! I've found something!" he shouted. A glance at Mariel told him that she was swaying as if her feet would no longer support her weight. He rushed back to her and slid a supporting arm around her shoulders.

"Come on, you can make it. It's a cave, and inside it looks dry."

Wordlessly she let him propel her to the opening, and he carefully took the baby and handed her the flashlight to light her way. She stumbled once as she tried to climb into the opening, which formed a downward chute ending in the larger room of the cave. He felt helpless to assist her, and, since she was carrying the flashlight, he couldn't see her. All was dark.

Light returned when Mariel finally dragged herself into the cave. Carefully shielding the baby's face from the prickly brambles, Jake crawled through the chute. He literally fell into the cave, regaining his balance by grabbing a projecting overhang near the entrance.

The cave was about a foot higher than his six feet, and, judging from the evidence of old camp fires, a place where other people had found shelter in the past. It was dank and damp and smelled of wood smoke, but their having found it was nevertheless a kind of miracle.

The baby stirred against his chest. Mariel sprawled on the sand floor, clutching the flashlight.

Safe, Jake thought. *We're safe.*

Chapter Three

Mariel was shivering violently. A thread of blood trickled down the side of her face from a scratch inflicted by the brambles. She slumped against the smoke-blackened wall of the cave, scarcely able to sit up.

"Mariel? Are you all right? Mariel?" Jake crouched beside her, and the baby in his arms whimpered.

Mariel couldn't answer. She had thoughts, but they wouldn't shape themselves into words. She was thinking *dry,* and *hungry,* and *baby,* and then, finally, *What should we do about the baby?* which made her, with the utmost effort, focus her blurred vision on Jake and the infant nestled in his arms.

"Can you hold her for a minute?" Jake was saying urgently.

With difficulty, Mariel adjusted her position to form a lap, her gaze locked on Jake's. With his face only inches from hers, she was all too aware of the complexity of the emotions flooding his dark eyes. In that moment she wanted nothing more than to sink into their warm depths, but she denied herself that comfort. Right now, there was the baby to think about.

The infant was thrashing her head fretfully from side to side, and her tiny lips were tinted blue. Jake was alarmed about her condition. He had expected her to be rosy and pink, the way she had been when they found her.

"You can't hold the baby against your wet coat," Jake said. Mariel fumbled with her coat buttons with weak fingers until Jake said, "Let me."

Cradling the baby in the crook of one arm, he shed his soggy glove and, one after the other, slid the buttons through their buttonholes. Under her coat, Mariel wore a white lamb's wool sweater that buttoned up the front. The collar of the sweater was damp, but the rest of it was warm and dry. She wore corduroy slacks, and Jake carefully laid the baby in her lap.

Jake didn't know who worried him most, the baby or Mariel. The thing was, neither of them was in good shape. Mariel, with her difficulty in unbuttoning her coat and her vague, slurred speech, was showing symptoms of hypothermia, and as a camper from way back, Jake knew the dangers. Hypothermia, subnormal body temperature, could kill.

He had to raise her body temperature, and the baby's, too. Mariel was a small woman, fine-boned, with little body fat to keep her warm. The shivering would help, it was a good sign, but it wasn't enough.

Mariel's scarf had fallen away to reveal a mass of pale curls tumbling across her shoulders. The scratch on her face was still bleeding, and without thinking, Jake reached out to rub the blood away. His thumb caressed her cheek, and if she hadn't been shivering so much he might have forgotten his purpose. At the moment, all he wanted to think about was the rose-petal texture of her skin.

"The baby," she whispered.

Jake slid his hands between the tiny body and Mariel's thighs. The baby began to wail, and Mariel made a nest of her arms. As soon as the baby felt Mariel's warmth, she quieted.

"Her blanket is so wet," Mariel said, but the words gave Jake hope—if not for the child, at least for Mariel. She was thinking, and that was a good sign.

Jake stripped the baby's blanket away. A quick inspection told him that the child's long flannel nightgown was damp around the bottom, but dry everywhere else, so he decided it was safe for the baby to wear. But he knew he'd better check Mariel's clothes, too.

"Jake," she said, moistening her lips with her tongue in a gesture that was unconsciously erotic. "I want to hold the baby next to my skin. We could warm each other."

"You want me to unbutton your sweater?" he asked.

"Please." She plucked at the tiny mother-of-pearl buttons marching in a straight row down her sweater front, but it was clear that she didn't have the strength to undo them herself.

Jake hesitated.

"Can you help?" she asked. Slowly he reached out and slid the top button out of its buttonhole. Damn, but the skin of her throat was soft.

It didn't take him long to part the sides of her sweater. Her bra seemed to be made out of cobwebs; he could see through it to the pale pink nipples, puckered from the cold. Mariel was exceptionally well endowed for a small woman, and Jake looked away, entirely unnerved by what the sight of her did to him. He wanted her. It was crazy. In her present state, he could easily take advantage of her, but of course he wouldn't. If only she weren't so beautiful and so desirable and so spirited; if only he weren't so powerfully attracted to her.

He forced himself to attend to business. He slid his arms under the baby and lifted it to Mariel's chest, guiding her arms around it. The baby hid her breasts, and he sighed in temporary relief.

He felt the bottoms of the blue corduroy pants that Mariel wore. The cuffs were cold and wet. He slid his hand upward to check the extent of the dampness, noting that she stiffened slightly as his hand went higher.

Her slacks were wet to the knee. "You're going to have to take these off," he said.

"Wh-what?"

"Take off those slacks. In your condition, it could be deadly to wear wet clothes," he said, clipping his words. He wasn't sure he was making any sense to her; hypothermia victims sometimes lacked judgment and reasoning power.

Mariel's only response was uncontrolled shivering, and that, added to the fact that she obviously was unable to do anything for herself, told Jake that he'd better act swiftly.

"I'm going to pull off your boots and socks and hang them up to dry," he told her. Mariel made no objection, and he slid the boots off her feet, then her cotton socks. Her feet were slim and white, dainty and well formed.

"Now the slacks," he said, reaching under her raincoat. "I'm going to pull these down over your hips. Help if you can."

He unfastened her belt buckle and yanked at the zipper, which immediately caught on a lace flounce in her underpants.

Swearing, Jake wiggled the zipper fastener, which refused to let go. It was firmly stuck.

He glanced at Mariel. Her eyes were open. She was watching him, her chin resting on the baby's head.

"Just what I need," he said tightly. "Another problem."

"Go ahead and rip it if you must," she said, looking embarrassed. He couldn't imagine *why* she would feel embarrassed. She was beautiful, her skin sweetly scented and inviting, her abdomen gently rounded between her hipbones. The triangle of lace that was giving him so much trouble did little to hide the pale curls beneath.

To his relief, when he again tried easing the zipper pull down the slide, the lace sprang free without tearing. In a moment Jake was shimmying the corduroy over Mariel's hipbones. She lifted her hips slightly, her eyes closed.

Jake found it difficult to look at her as if she were an object instead of an attractive woman with considerable sex appeal. He wasn't prepared for the way the sight of her body sent lightning sparking along every one of his nerve endings, and he had to resist to the fullest his impulse to let his fingers stray from their task.

"Tough duty," she said, as he was hanging her corduroys from a convenient rock projection, and he realized that she was trying to make light of the situation for his sake, as well as hers. When he turned back to her, she had already wrapped herself modestly in her coat. Her feet looked shriveled and cold, and that reminded him of his next task.

"I've got to build a fire right away," he said. Mariel's only reply was a nod.

Jake inspected their shelter. The cave was about seven feet wide and perhaps ten feet deep, its walls ledged, its floor a combination of rock and sand. As it played across the back of the cave, the beam of the flashlight picked out a small stack of firewood, which Jake knew was their salvation. It would be impossible to find dry wood outside.

He looked back at Mariel. She was still shivering, but not as violently as before. Her hair was drying in soft, fetching ringlets around her face; the folds of her coat barely hinted at the sweet curves of her body.

Tough duty, indeed, he thought to himself. It was going to be very hard for him to keep his behavior within the bounds of respectability. Mariel Evans was an exceptionally lovely woman. And he was a healthy, red-blooded American male.

MARIEL KEPT her eyes closed while Jake went about the serious business of building a fire. She was shaken by the force of her feelings. Jake's hands had touched her skin as little as possible, and yet, as innocent as his touch had been, she felt physically disturbed by it.

The warmth of the baby against her breasts felt oddly erotic. Jake's scent drifted up from the baby's skin—a woodsy after-shave underlaid by the pungent odor of wet wool. The baby's head pressed tightly against a nipple, engendering a heat that coursed through her veins and made her think about the crisp efficiency of Jake's hands as they had undressed her. The cold must have affected her in a very strange way. Who else in this predicament would be fantasizing about a man whom she had met only hours ago?

For once she regretted her penchant for wispy underwear. It was her secret indulgence. Now she thought she

would have been better off with something utilitarian
and opaque. Jake had gotten an eyeful, despite his
feigned disinterest.

The baby made little snuffling noises, and she realized suddenly that it was rooting against her bare skin,
searching for something to eat. It was basic instinct for
a baby to do this, she figured. But suddenly she couldn't
bear the stimulation of the warm, seeking mouth
against her breast, and she abruptly changed position
so that the baby's face rested against the soft cable knit
of her sweater.

"I need something to use for tinder," Jake said,
breaking into her thoughts.

Mariel was grateful for this reminder of practical
matters. "Look in my bag. There's a notepad I seldom
use."

Jake found the pad and crushed the paper into wads.
When he dug into his pack and emerged with matches
in a waterproof canister, Mariel thanked her lucky stars
that she was sharing this experience with an outdoorsy
man who had some survival skills.

The tinder caught fire, and the flames, carefully nur-
tured by Jake, spread to the kindling. Mariel watched
him as he blew on the flames, coaxing them to life. His
face was rugged, his nose blunt, his mouth mobile. Not
like the baby's tiny rosebud mouth, but well-shaped, the
lower lip slightly pendulous, the upper one deeply
grooved.

He saw her watching him, but made no comment.
When the fire was burning brightly, sending tongues of
yellow flame leaping toward the ceiling of the cave, he
sat up and removed his boots and wet socks, laying the
socks on a ledge above the fire to dry. "How are you
feeling?" he asked gruffly.

"Better."

He picked up her hand and closed his fingers around her wrist. "I want to check your pulse. I'm worried about you." He kept his eyes on his watch, and Mariel felt her pulse beating against his fingertips.

"You're fine," he said finally. He dropped her wrist and took a thermos from his pack. He poured milk into the metal cap and heated it over the flames. Mariel slid her feet even closer to the fire and flexed her toes in pleasure.

"Here," Jake said gruffly, holding out the cup of warm milk.

"We should save it for the baby."

"You need it. I'll heat some for her after you're through," he told her.

But Mariel's hand shook so much that she couldn't wrap her fingers around the cup.

"I'll help." Leaning toward her, Jake placed his hand over hers and guided the cup to her lips. She drank slowly, the milk warming her as it went down. It was no more than two or three ounces, but Mariel immediately began to feel stronger, and soon she stopped shivering. The fire was a roaring blaze now, the smoke disappearing into a crack in the cave's ceiling.

Jake's expression was unreadable in the firelight. He knelt beside her, his jacket open to reveal a gray turtleneck sweater that defined the firm pectoral muscles underneath. Mariel drew a long, deep breath, hoping to infuse her addled brain with clarity and judgment. The tingle she felt was not due to the return of warmth to her half-frozen limbs; it was directly attributable to the presence of Jake Travis.

She pulled herself together when the baby began to whimper. "We'd better feed her," she told him, gazing at the bundle in her arms. She wondered what, if any, effect exposure to the cold had had on the child. She looked better now, Mariel thought.

"Aren't babies supposed to drink formula from a can, not cow's milk?" Jake asked anxiously.

"We don't have any formula," she reminded him.

"I don't want to harm the baby, that's all," he said.

For someone who had reacted with anger at his first sight of the baby, Jake had softened quite a bit. He looked so concerned that Mariel's heart went out to him.

"We're talking survival here. We have no choice," she said.

"How much milk would a baby drink at one feeding, anyway?"

"I have no idea," Mariel admitted. They both looked at the baby, trying to assess her capacity.

"She's not very big. Her stomach couldn't hold much," Jake said.

"Three ounces?"

"Maybe," he agreed. "How are we going to feed her?"

"I don't know."

They looked at each other blankly.

"Maybe if we soaked a piece of cloth in the milk, she could suck on it. I saw that in a movie once. Trouble is, they were feeding motherless puppies," Jake said ruefully.

"I carry eyedrops in my purse," Mariel said. "Maybe the eyedropper?"

"It might work."

"Get it, please. There's an unopened package of eyedrops in my cosmetic bag," she said. The baby began to cry, the noise ricocheting off the cave's walls so that no more discussion was possible.

"This must be it," Jake said, holding the box aloft. He tore off the cellophane wrapper.

Mariel raised her voice to be heard over the baby's wails. "The eyedropper should be wrapped in plastic," she said.

Jake held it up for her inspection. "Is it sterile?"

"It says so on the box," she said. "How about the milk? Do you suppose it needs to be sterilized?" She had a vague memory from her childhood of a neighbor boiling baby bottles in a big pan on her stove. She didn't know if anyone still did that.

"Does milk have a lot of germs?"

Mariel didn't know. She shrugged her shoulders.

"I could boil the milk in my thermos lid," he said. "That might take care of it."

"What about the taste? I think boiled milk tastes awful."

"We don't know if she'll drink cow's milk anyway, boiled or unboiled," Jake said. They both regarded the baby, whose face was red from crying. She looked furious.

"If she doesn't eat something, she'll die," Mariel said.

"So back to the question—do we boil the milk?"

Mariel tried to think. She had friends who had babies, but she'd never paid much attention to their care. It seemed to her that her friend Carole had fed her baby canned baby formula, then switched to cow's milk poured directly into the baby bottle from a milk bottle kept in the refrigerator. Had that been at three months? Or had the baby been on formula for six months?

Mariel couldn't recall. She also didn't know the age of this baby, who appeared to be only a month or two old. But then, Mariel didn't know anything about babies. Her college degrees hadn't prepared her for a situation like this one. All she knew was that they'd better make a fast decision.

She decided. "We'll warm the milk and give it to her as it is, but first, you'd better sterilize the thermos lid by boiling water in it, don't you think?" she asked Jake.

"I don't know what I think," he said through tight lips. "Mostly what I think is that we're ill-equipped to take care of a kid."

"I couldn't agree with you more," Mariel said, failing to control the edginess in her tone.

Jake went outside for water. While he was boiling it in the metal lid, the baby's crying grew louder and more frantic, straining their frayed nerves to the breaking point.

"Can't you keep her quiet?" Jake asked sharply.

"I'm trying," said Mariel over the din. "Hurry up, will you?"

Jake growled, "I'm doing this as fast as I can," whereupon Mariel regretted her own testiness. She turned her attention to the baby again, smoothing the golden hair, rubbing the little back under the nightgown, all to no avail. The baby was hungry, and that was that.

Jake poured out the boiled water, since there was nowhere to keep it, and sniffed the thermos lid. Mariel almost smiled, thinking that smelling it wasn't going to tell him if germs were present, germs not necessarily having odors.

Anyway, what kind of germs were they worried about? Didn't babies put all kinds of things in their mouths, such as key chains that had dropped on the floor, and the dog's chewy pieces of rawhide? And didn't most babies survive such adventures? Someday Mariel would look up the answers to all these questions. She realized that baby care was a great gap in her knowledge.

Jake, apparently satisfied that the lid from his thermos was clean enough, heated a bit of milk and drew some of it into the eyedropper.

"Here," he said, carefully transferring the dropper to Mariel's outstretched hand. She smiled a silent thank-you when their hands touched.

With Jake watching over her shoulder, Mariel dribbled a few drops of milk into the baby's open mouth. The infant stopped crying immediately and looked mystified.

"There, that's better, isn't it?" crooned Mariel. The baby closed her lips around the eyedropper, her eyes never leaving Mariel's face.

The dropper wasn't the best feeding apparatus in the world, because it wasn't suited for sucking, something that the baby expected to be able to do. As fast as Mariel filled the eyedropper, the baby drank, but it was frustrating to watch the baby trying to suck on the hard plastic tube and to listen to her fussing while Mariel refilled it.

"Damned inefficient," Jake said.

Mariel glared at him. "Would you like to try it?"

"No, no," he said, backing away. He watched them for a few more moments. "I feel helpless," he said, giving her the idea that it was an admission that he seldom, if ever, made. "Usually when something needs doing, I can make something to do the job. I'm a fair plumber, a pretty good electrician, and a bang-up carpenter. This has me stumped.''

"Me too," she offered, and he grinned at her.

After she had swallowed three or four ounces of milk, the baby stopped eating and puckered her little face as if she were going to cry again.

"Uh-oh," said Jake. "I think something's wrong."

"She has to be burped."

"Burped? How?"

"She's supposed to be patted on the back. I think it brings up the air bubbles."

"Give her to me. I'll try it."

Carefully he took the baby from Mariel.

"You'll have to drape her over your shoulder," Mariel said.

"There, there," Jake said to the baby in a soothing voice.

"She's waiting for you to do something," Mariel told him. She wanted to giggle; Jake, so masculine and rugged, looked absurd with the baby slung over his shoulder. He was holding her as if she were a sack of wood chips.

Jake thumped the baby between the shoulder blades, producing nothing but a startled look.

"Not so hard," Mariel hastened to say, and when Jake experimented with a few tentative taps, the baby obliged by producing a sonorous belch.

"That was pretty good, wasn't it?" Jake asked, sounding smug.

"Better than I could have done," Mariel said, meaning it.

The immediate problem of hunger solved, Mariel reached over and gingerly felt the baby's diaper.

"She's sopping wet."

"Nowhere in this cave have I found a stack of diapers. Have I?" Jake said to the baby, who yawned.

"If my scarf weren't so wet, we might use it as a diaper," Mariel said, though she wasn't at all sure about it's suitability.

The discarded scarf lay in a damp heap on the sand, its fringe clumped together. "It's too stiff and woolly. Babies' diapers need to be soft, like cotton. At least I know that much," Jake said. He was still jaunty from his success at bringing up the baby's air bubble.

"Well, we've got to think of something," Mariel said, staring pensively at the baby, who looked back at her unblinkingly and with great interest. There was trust in that gaze, and Mariel wondered how on earth they were going to meet the complex needs of an infant using only the things they had on hand.

"I know," Jake said suddenly.

"What?"

"What we can use for diapers."

"Is it bigger than a breadbox?" Mariel asked, with more than a hint of sarcasm.

"Never mind. Here, take the baby and turn your head," he told her.

She took the baby, but what he'd said didn't register until he began unbuckling his belt.

"You're not going to take off your clothes?" Mariel blurted out.

"Only my long johns. They'll make good diapers," he replied, seemingly unperturbed.

"Oh," Mariel said faintly. There was nowhere in this cave where he could go for privacy. He'd have to take his pants off in front of her.

"Don't worry—I'm wearing briefs underneath. I often dress warmly at this time of year. In my job, I sometimes have to work in unheated areas."

Mariel could have sworn that she saw the hint of a grin. "Don't we have something else we can use?" she asked skeptically.

"Do you have a better idea, Mariel?"

She realized the futility and folly of objecting to what he had in mind. "No. *No.* It sounds fine. Just do it, okay?"

"Don't look at me, if it'll embarrass you," he said, mollified.

Mariel turned her head away and tried to ignore the sounds of his undressing until she discovered that, by squinting out of the corners of her eyes, she could see him clearly by the light of the fire.

First he shucked off his boots, and then his wool socks, which he hung to dry above the fire. Then, slowly and deliberately, he unbuckled his belt.

She managed to close her eyes before he glanced sharply in her direction, but at the sound of the zipper, she peeked under her lids.

Jake's worn jeans were molded to his body as if they had grown there, and their dampness revealed the firmness of his thighs, the compact curves of his buttocks.

As graceful as a panther, he stepped out of the jeans and dropped them onto the ledge next to his socks. As he pulled down his white cotton-knit long johns, Mariel saw that his thighs were muscled and lightly furred with dark hair. The briefs he wore underneath were brief indeed, revealing a tapering V of hair that disappeared under the waistband, near the well-defined bulge below. She could hardly pull her eyes away as he stood, clad only in turtleneck and briefs, the hard contours of his body limned by firelight and gilded by its glow.

She caught her breath at the sight of him, thinking that she'd never seen a man who so exuded sexuality. Even here, in this miserable cave, Jake Travis had that indefinable animal magnetism that made woman weak, and though it could be argued that she was already weak, her ordeal hadn't caused the catch in her throat when she looked at him, or the tension vibrating just below her skin.

She had been aware of his arresting good looks from the moment they met. His mere touch had been enough to banish her cold-induced stupor. Now that she was being treated to the full impact of his physical presence, she was brought up short by a confusing tangle of emotions.

He caught her staring at him. It might have been her imagination, but he seemed to draw himself up to his full height, a desirable male exhibiting himself more fully to a female who was clearly admiring.

"I thought you weren't planning to look," he said, sounding amused.

"I'm not *looking*," she lied. "I have to aim my eyes somewhere, after all."

"I never thought about it that way," he said, but she knew he was laughing at her.

Let him, she told herself. She'd have had to be deaf, dumb and blind to ignore the chemistry between them, but she was well aware that in this survival situation it could only make things more difficult.

"I think I'll leave my jeans beside the fire until they dry," he said. She made no comment.

Jake anchored his jeans to a ledge above the fire with a rock, and then he knelt and withdrew a knife from his pack, his movements swift and economical. The fire-light emphasized the braided muscles of his thighs and calves as he squatted and spread his discarded long johns across his knees. His hair was dark, and longer than she had thought at first; it had sprung into a shining frame for his face. Intent on his task, he didn't look up, seeming totally unaware that she was observing him so closely.

There was something strange and elemental in this scene. Mariel could almost imagine that they were cave dwellers in some ancient age, making do with what was available. He was the provider and she the mother of the child who slept in her arms, snug and warm....

She awoke with a start. Jake was shaking her arm, his face contorted with fear.

"Don't go to sleep!" he said.

"I only—"

"It's all right," he said, the sparks fading from his eyes and his shoulders slumping when he realized that she had only been drowsing.

"I must have dropped off for a moment," she began, but he silenced her with a finger across her lips.

"One moment you were wide awake, watching me work, and the next minute your head was nodding and you didn't hear me say your name. I thought—"

"I'm fine," she said. She shifted her position to avoid the rock that was biting into her backbone, wondering how she could have slept while so uncomfortable.

He checked her pulse, holding tight to her wrist. "Normal," he pronounced.

"I told you I'm okay," she said.

"I'm still worried about hypothermia. You shouldn't sleep yet—it could be dangerous."

"I'll try to stay awake," she promised. She nearly told him about the appearance of the man with the white bushy beard in the woods earlier, when she had almost fallen asleep. Jake didn't seem to be in the mood to hear a fanciful story, but she couldn't help musing over what she had seen. Was the little man real? Or had he been a dream?

Jake went back to the fire, squatting there as he contemplated the destruction of his long underwear.

"I wonder what size a diaper is," he mused.

"She's a small baby," Mariel answered. "Cut them into large pieces, and we'll fold them to the size we need." The baby in her arms slept openmouthed, her small puffs of breath stirring the fuzz of Mariel's sweater. Her upturned nose was smaller than the tip of Mariel's thumb, and her cheeks were fat and round. She looked like a little cherub, and already Mariel knew that if it were necessary, she wouldn't hesitate to put her life on the line for this baby.

She would have liked to ask Jake if he felt the same way, but he was making short work of cutting up his long johns, holding up the resulting pieces of fabric for her approval.

"Okay," she said when he had finished. "Let's change her diaper."

"You deserve the honors," Jake said.

"I've never diapered a baby."

"Neither have I," he confessed.

Mariel sighed. "All right, I'll try. We need a clean place to lay her down," she said.

There was only the sandy floor. "Here," Jake said, spreading his jacket over the sand. The inside was warm and dry, and Mariel carefully lifted the baby out of her coat and laid her on the jacket lining. She quickly closed her sweater over her breasts, but not before Jake saw a tantalizing glimpse of her lacy bra.

Mariel unpinned the diaper. The baby awoke, fussed briefly, then saw Mariel's face and began to kick and coo.

"She acts as if life's going on as usual," commented Jake, who looked on from above, his arms folded over his chest.

"Maybe that's why she's here. To remind us that it should," Mariel said briskly, sliding the clean white cotton knit beneath the baby's buttocks.

Mariel's observation took Jake by surprise. For one thing, it made him look at this situation in a new way. For another, it clued him in to Mariel's thought processes. He liked her knack for putting a positive spin on things.

"There," Mariel said, smiling down at the baby. The child waved her fists in the air, and Mariel gathered her into her arms. "Is her blanket dry yet?"

Jake checked. "Nope," he said, hoping that Mariel would open her sweater again.

While he was thinking that, Mariel said, "You'd better put this dirty diaper outside. If only we had something to wash it in, like a pan of some kind."

Jake went back to the stack of firewood and emerged from the shadows triumphantly, a beat-up old tin pot in his hand. The bottom was fire-blackened, but as far as Jake could see, it didn't have any holes.

"I'll set it out to catch water," Jake said, and, to his disappointment, Mariel had already snuggled the baby inside her sweater when he returned.

"Are you warm enough?" he asked her.

She nodded, barely able to keep her eyes open.

Jake regarded her for a moment. Her cheeks were rosy again, and she had brushed her hair behind her ears. She had Dresden-doll coloring, delicate and comely, and her eyes sparkled. It was all he could do not to bend over and kiss her pink lips.

He did lean closer, using the baby as an excuse. "She's pretty, isn't she?" he asked, but he wasn't looking at the baby. He was studying the cleft in Mariel's chin, hoping she wouldn't notice.

"She's a wonderful baby," Mariel agreed. "You like her, don't you?" She watched Jake anxiously for his response. Somehow it seemed important that he love this infant, that he harbor the same tender feelings toward her that she did.

Jake didn't answer right away. "She's okay, I guess," he said reluctantly, but from his tone of voice Mariel knew that he was as taken with the baby as she was.

They sat silently, watching the baby breathe. Smoke curled up from the fire toward some unseen outlet in the cave roof, and sparks danced in an occasional gust of wind that penetrated the sheltering brambles at the entrance. Outside, the sleet continued to fall, holding them prisoner.

"There's half a sandwich in my pack," Jake said quietly.

"We'll split it," Mariel said, and soon he had cut the sandwich into two portions and was handing one to her. Jake heated water in the thermos cap, and they sipped alternately from it.

"I have an apple, too. We can eat it in the morning," Jake said.

Mariel nodded, and after a while he saw her head falling to one side. She jerked it up again.

"Let's talk, so you won't go to sleep," he said.

"You talk," she said.

"That would put you to sleep for sure. Tell me about where you live, your family, your job."

Mariel sighed and shifted position again. "I live in an apartment with a bay window overlooking a garden—" she began, but he interrupted her.

"What kind of garden? Vegetables? Flowers?"

"Both, but I love the flowers best. Do you know that the Victorians wrote a language of the flowers? Mistletoe, for instance. It means 'Give me a kiss.'" She stopped talking suddenly, looking flustered.

To fill the gap in the conversation, Jake said, "Is your apartment big? Small?"

"Two bedrooms. And it's not far from the museum where I work," she told him.

"I never knew anyone who was a folklorist."

"I'm surprised. In this part of Virginia, there are probably all kinds of stories the local people tell, legends to be collected."

"Maybe so. I don't run into them much, that's all. I've only been in Virginia for a short time—moved here from Atlanta around Christmastime three years ago, in fact. I think I left Atlanta mostly *because* it was Christmas, because that way I could avoid all the hoopla that I wasn't part of," Jake said.

"Well, my family was small, since I was an only child, but I always loved the 'hoopla,'" said Mariel.

"Must be nice," Jake said noncommittally.

"I guess I was spoiled, in a way. Everything I wished for—no matter how silly—somehow came true at Christmas. A bicycle once, a puppy another year, my grandparents flying in for a visit—all were wishes of mine."

"I think I would have wished for a Lamborghini when I was sixteen, and maybe a football scholarship, even though I never played," Jake said with a grin.

"Well, my wishes had to be within reason. I mean, it wouldn't have done any good to wish for the moon on a silver platter, because it's an impossibility."

"These three wishes you're always making... Now that you're an adult, don't you feel ridiculous doing it?" he asked curiously.

"Why would I? Wishes *can* come true, Jake. Magic *can* happen. There *are* such things as miracles," she said.

"Hogwash," he said amiably.

"Hogwash! Listen, Jake Travis, it was no mere co-incidence that you found this cave when we needed it. Or that we happened along when the baby needed us. And let me ask you this—how often do you have milk left in your thermos after lunch?"

His eyes shone mischievously as he bent to stir the fire. "Often, in fact. Sometimes the guys on the job go to a convenience store and pick up a six-pack of cola. Or, like today, it's cold and somebody offers us a hot drink for lunch," he said.

"Okay, so I struck out on that last one. But there's still the cave and the baby. Don't forget that," she said.

"It's probably safe for you to sleep now."

"You're ready to shut me up, right?" she asked him with a glint of humor.

"Not exactly," he hedged, thinking that he could go on listening to her high musical voice all night long. She had a way of talking that slid up and down the scales, a sound most pleasing to the ear. To his ear, at any rate.

"I'm glad to hear that. Tomorrow I may want to talk a lot more. You're a good listener, Jake."

It was a compliment he hadn't heard before, or at least couldn't remember hearing, which amounted to the same thing. He wasn't sure if he should say thank you, so he only nodded his head slightly. Mariel wasn't like any women he knew; most of them were practical and down-to-earth. Not that Mariel wasn't, but she had another, more evanescent quality too, one that he couldn't quite put his finger on. She had a lot of charm, that was for sure.

"There's no place to stretch out except on the sand. If you'd like, I'll hold the baby while you get settled," he said.

"At least we're not out in the cold," she answered as he took the child in his arms.

"And to think it's all because of magic," he said, teasing her.

"I'm glad you're starting to think my way," she tossed back, her eyes sparkling at him, and he knew that she knew that he didn't really believe, and that it was all right. He wouldn't put it past her to work on him some more, and for some reason, he was actually looking forward to it, to sparring with her, to watching her expressive face as she spoke so earnestly.

"I'm ready," she said when she had arranged herself on the sand, and Jake handed the child to her. Mariel tucked the baby inside her sweater again and lay down on her side, flexing her legs to curve her body protectively around the child and pillowing her head on her tote bag.

"Aren't you going to sleep?" she asked, looking up at him. Her eyes were bright and glowing.

The two of them had established a camaraderie, a rapport. He hoped she felt it as strongly as he did.

"I'm going to sit up for a while. I want to keep an eye on the fire," he said, because he knew that he could not lie down beside her without touching her.

The fire crackled and spit, and he saw Mariel tenderly stroking the pale golden hair on the baby's head. He wished it was him she was comforting.

Mariel seemed to represent everything that he didn't have in his life, everything that other people lived for, not him. He wasn't normally a sentimental guy, so maybe it was that she had taken such care to remind him of the Christmas season, or maybe it was that she looked so Madonna-like with the baby in her arms. He tried to swallow the lump in his throat, but it wouldn't go away.

When Mariel was asleep, Jake got up and brought in the thermos cap, which he had set out earlier to catch water. He heated the water and sipped it slowly, resting on his haunches. After a while, he dropped another log on the fire and lay down as far from Mariel and the baby as he deemed necessary, wrapped in his wool jacket. He was sleeping lightly when he heard Mariel moan. He shot up, instantly alert.

"Mariel?" he said.

"Cold," she muttered, and was quiet.

He felt her corduroys, which were still hanging from the ledge, but they were still damp. All Jake could think of to do was what he had wanted to do all along. He nestled himself against the back of Mariel's body and twined his legs around hers for warmth. She murmured something indistinct, and he reached under her coat and slid his warm hands up along her rib cage. Her ribs seemed not like mere bones, but like a house to enclose her beating heart.

Her heart throbbed beneath his fingertips, and his thumbs brushed the soft underside of her breasts. After a few moments, his breathing automatically synchronized with hers. He smelled the wildflower scent of Mariel's shampoo, blended with the sweet, milky fragrance of the baby, and it was all he could do not to bury his face in the nape of Mariel's neck.

Jake didn't know if Mariel realized he was there, but it didn't matter. All that mattered was her warmth, and her softness, and that neither of them was alone in the dark.

Chapter Four

When Mariel awoke, she didn't know where she was. Her joints and muscles hurt, and a baby was crying.

She opened her eyes. A few feet away, glowing coals were a red eye in the dark.

All at once, Mariel remembered. The accident. Their trek along the icy road. The baby. The cave. Her exhaustion. And Jake. Where was he?

Something moved behind her, and she stiffened in alarm before she realized that it was Jake and that his legs were wrapped around hers. She twisted away as he sat up and said in a groggy tone, "Maybe the baby's hungry." He went to stir the fire, and it blazed brighter.

"You were—" she began.

"I was keeping you warm. You were cold."

"I was asleep," she said, with as much dignity as she could muster.

"So was I," he said. He got up and felt his jeans, which still hung by the fire. They were still wet, and he moved them closer to the flames, his back toward her.

"I didn't ask you to keep me warm," Mariel said.

"You cried out in your sleep." He turned and leveled a serious gaze at her. "I was only trying to help."

Mariel didn't know whether to thank him or not, but at that moment the baby started wailing at the top of her lungs. Thankful for the distraction, Mariel sat up and studied the infant. She was putting all her energy into screaming, and one tiny pink foot had escaped the nightgown.

Jake was bringing a fresh log for the fire. "Jessica," Mariel said, raising her voice over the baby's cries. "I'm going to call her Jessica."

Jake looked harried. "Is that the most important thing you can think about, with her carrying on like that?" he asked, his eyebrows lifting.

"She has to have a name. We can't keep calling her 'the baby,'" said Mariel. Carefully she spread the baby on her lap and checked the diaper. Soaked. No wonder she was crying.

Jake had already poured milk into the metal cap and set it on a hot rock to warm.

"Diaper time again," Mariel said. Jake's hair was standing up in clumps, and he needed a shave. She didn't look so terrific, either, she imagined. She felt grungy and disheveled, and she needed to relieve herself.

Jake brought another piece of his long johns, took off his jacket, and spread it out. Mariel laid the baby— *Jessica*, she reminded herself—on it.

Jake felt one of the baby's arms. "She's cold. We should keep her covered while you're doing this," he said. He brought the pink blanket, which was finally dry, and folded it across Jessica, who was punching her arms and legs into the air as if against an unseen assailant.

"Your turn for this chore," she said to Jake above the noise. His mouth dropped open.

"I can't—"

"Of course you can," she said, smiling encouragingly.

"I told you, I've never changed a diaper," he said in bewilderment.

"Neither had I until last night," she reminded him.

"But she's kicking," he said, eyeing Jessica's flailing legs. He looked up at Mariel, who had started pulling on her boots while he was voicing his objections. "Where are you going?" he demanded.

"Out." She stood up, surprised that she felt so strong. Her knees gave nary a wobble. She took a few experimental steps, testing them out.

"Why are you going out?"

Mariel regarded him with exasperation.

"I don't see any facilities in here," she pointed out.

It was almost comical, the way he clamped his mouth shut.

"Oh," he said. "Well, uh, when you get outside the cave, turn to your left. There's a chunk of rock that provides shelter from the wind. And you'd better take the flashlight," he said. He was still looking at Jessica's wet diaper, steeling himself to remove it.

She bent, picked up the flashlight, and said sweetly, "Be careful not to stick her with a pin, won't you?" She was rewarded by a perplexed expression, and it was all she could do to keep from laughing when she emerged from the cave.

It had stopped sleeting, but at this predawn hour, it was still dark. Mariel found the boulder, took care of business and, mindful of the scratch on her face, negotiated the brambles at the cave entrance with care. Once safely inside, she switched off the flashlight and sat down beside Jake.

"How'd you do?" she asked. He was squeezing a dropperful of milk into Jessica's mouth, concentrating mightily on the task.

"It'd be a lot easier if you could nail diapers on kids. I didn't poke *her* with the pin, but I stuck myself." He held up his pricked finger for her to see.

"But you survived," she pointed out.

"Barely. So did the baby—barely. That was supposed to be a pun," he said.

"Cute, Jake. Very cute. How much milk is left, by the way?" she asked.

"A few ounces. I'm not going to give her much this feeding. We'll need some for the morning."

"What time is it now?"

"Three o'clock in the morning."

"It doesn't seem like it. I feel so wide awake," Mariel said. She drew her bare legs under her for warmth and watched Jake's hands as they ministered so gently to the baby. They were capable hands, and she would trust them with her life. In fact, she had. She felt a warming toward him and wondered how he felt about her.

"Why did you name her Jessica?" Jake asked.

Mariel was surprised. She hadn't expected conversation. "I've always like the name," she told him.

"Any special reason?"

"When I was in high school, dreaming about a home and family, as many girls do, I chose the names for all four of my children," she said.

He lifted his head and grinned at her. "Four?"

"I was going to have a station wagon, and I wanted to fill it with kids. I'd take them to swimming lessons in the summer, to children's concerts in the park, and all kinds of things. Jessica, Mark, Joanna and Matthew.

Those were their names. But—" she sighed "—I never bought that station wagon."

"Regrets?"

"A few. I love my job. I just wish there was something *more.*"

"Like a Jessica?" he probed, glancing at her.

"I've thought about becoming a single mother. I haven't quite figured out how, that's all."

"Shouldn't be too hard, for a woman who looks like you," he said quietly.

"Oh, that's not the problem. But there are only so many ways to go about acquiring a child. If a single woman wants a baby, she can be artificially inseminated, but it's too expensive for me to contemplate. Or she can ask a male friend to be the father, but then, what if he expects to be part of the child's life, as he has every right to do? Would I have to invite him to birthday parties and Christmas dinners for the next twenty years? I've never known a man that I wanted to put up with for that long. So that leaves adoption," she said.

Jake fed Jessica the last drops of milk from the thermos cap. "I guess you've thought about it a lot."

"And then I find a baby in the woods. It seems—it seems like a kind of gift," she said.

"She belongs to someone," Jake said, turning the drowsy infant over his shoulder.

"But to whom? And why was she there? It's almost as if someone knew we would come along to save her," Mariel said as Jessica twisted her head around to look at her. Jake was patting the baby's back, to no avail.

"She doesn't want to burp," he said.

"She will. Won't you, Jessica, darling? Come on, burp for us," coaxed Mariel.

As if on cue, Jessica brought up a bubble of air and triumphantly waved a fist in the air.

"Let me hold her for a while. You can go back to sleep," Jake said.

Mariel propped herself against the wall of the cave. "I'm not tired. I must have really been out of it before," she said. She was remembering how cozy and warm she'd felt; now she knew that it had been because of Jake's closeness. It had been his warmth, his body heat seeping through her clothes, making her comfortable, letting her sleep.

"You were dead to the world," Jake confirmed. He had derived great comfort from her. He'd have liked her to know that. And yet it seemed inappropriate to talk about it.

"It's stopped sleeting," Mariel said.

"Then we can get an early start. We should leave as soon as the sun rises," he replied.

"Sunrise is only a few hours away."

"That's why I think you should sleep," he said. "You'll need all your energy for whatever happens."

"What do you think will happen?" she asked, looking slightly alarmed.

"I don't know. But if anyone had predicted when we set out during the storm that we'd be spending the night in this cave while trying to figure out how to take care of an infant, I would have accused him of partaking of illegal hallucinogens."

"Have *you* ever done that?"

"No. What kind of question is that, anyway?" he said, halfway offended.

"One designed to find out about your habits."

"Not smart. Besides, I could have lied."

"You wouldn't."

"How do you know?"

"Because you aren't that kind of guy. You were upfront with me from the beginning by admitting that the accident was your fault, that your brakes didn't work. Any lawyer would caution you not to admit liability, but you had to tell the truth. It's in your nature," she said.

He found this conversation fascinating, not only because of where it was going, but also because it covered new territory. Usually women asked if he had been married, if he'd fathered any children, and if there was a serious relationship in his life. Also how much money he made; the answer often caused them to beat a hasty retreat.

"So," he said easily, massaging Jessica's back, "are you always so good at instant character analysis?"

"Most of the time. Men don't like it."

"Why?"

"They don't like being figured out."

"Do I?"

"You're humoring me, so you'll put up with it," she told him.

"Hmm..." he said, sliding the baby into his lap. He moved his forefinger back and forth in front of the tiny face, and the baby's Wedgwood-blue eyes tracked it.

"It's Christmas Eve day," Mariel said, stretching. "It doesn't seem much like it, does it?"

He shrugged. "What's the big deal?" he said.

She stared at him. "Well, tomorrow we will celebrate the birth of Christ, for one thing," she said. "Aren't you a Christian?"

"Supposedly. I lived in a couple of so-called Christian foster homes when I was a kid. They believed in 'Spare the rod, spoil the child,' which forever spoiled Christianity for me."

"They beat you?"

"Me and the other kids who lived there," he said.

Jessica was sound asleep in his lap. She looked sweet and innocent and supremely helpless.

"Well, my experience of religion was Sunday school and church picnics and marching in place in front of the pew when we sang 'Onward Christian Soldiers.' And later, serving as an acolyte and reading part of the Christmas Eve service. Besides," Mariel added, "I can't understand anyone who would hit a child."

"It shouldn't happen. Ever. For any reason," Jake said tersely.

"In my house, it wouldn't. I mean, if I were lucky enough to have a child." She gazed longingly at Jessica.

"If *I* had a child, I wouldn't fill her head with all this Christmas nonsense. Santa sliding down the chimney, bringing gifts for good little girls and boys. What if you've been good and there are no gifts?" Jake asked. He meant the question to be rhetorical, and he was surprised when Mariel shot back an answer.

"The child would be soured on the whole Christmas idea, right? Like you, right?"

"Right." The word was no more than a growl deep in his throat.

"Well," she said, "no matter what you think, it's still Christmas Eve day. And I'm going to keep the season, no matter what." To Jake that seemed like a silly statement, considering that they didn't know what the day would bring. He only hoped she wouldn't break into several choruses of "Deck the Halls with Boughs of Holly" while they were confined to this damn cave.

"I'm going to catch a few more Zs," he told her, thoroughly annoyed with all this sweetness and light.

"Maybe that's a good idea," she agreed, but he thought it was mostly because she didn't want to talk to him anymore.

"Who's going to hold the baby?" she asked.

"I will. In fact, I think we should sandwich her between us. The fire's getting low, and we only have a few sticks of firewood left. It's bound to get colder in here."

She seemed uncertain, looking at him out of the corners of wide eyes.

"Go ahead, lie down. I'll settle Jessica. It won't be much different from before," he said.

With one last, unfathomable look, Mariel lay down and pillowed her head on her tote bag, the way she had earlier. She jackknifed her knees and wrapped the folds of her coat close around her so that all Jake could see was the soles of her boots peeking out from under the fabric.

Carefully he wrapped the baby in the front of his coat; Jessica didn't even wake up. He slid down next to Mariel so that the baby occupied the space between her back and his chest.

"Comfortable?" he asked as he propped his head on his arm. Mariel shifted so that he felt the rounding of her derriere against his thighs. He was unprepared for his sudden arousal, and he leaned away from her under the guise of readjusting Jessica's blanket.

"Well, this isn't the Comfort Inn, you know," Mariel mumbled.

He didn't reply.

"Jake?"

"Hmm?"

"Did you remember to lock the door?"

He felt her shoulders shaking and realized that she was laughing. In a moment, he was laughing, too, and as he did, he realized that the burden of the situation had lightened with her mood.

In his experience, women always took everything so seriously. He had seldom come across one who could laugh in the face of adversity. He wanted to wrap his arms around her and pull her to him.

After a few moments, he heard Mariel's steady breathing. He should have slept, but he didn't. He was thinking that Mariel was a woman he'd like to get to know, and yet their backgrounds were so different. She was college-educated, and he wasn't. She was from a big city, and he was small-town. And if he cared about his own happiness, he'd better nip these thoughts in the bud.

THE GRAY SHAFTS OF LIGHT creeping in through the mouth of the cave woke Mariel first. She lay quietly, listening to Jake breathe. She felt Jessica resting snugly against her back, and she wondered if the bit of milk left in Jake's thermos would be enough for the baby's breakfast. One thing was certain—they would have to find civilization soon.

Civilization...people...home...At her apartment in Pittsburgh, the neighborhood kids would soon be knocking on her door, looking for handouts of candy canes. When she wasn't there, they would be disappointed. She always asked a few of them inside to help her decorate her tree. Would they tell their parents when she didn't answer their knocks? Would anyone think to notify the authorities that she was missing?

She wouldn't be missed at work; she was supposed to be on vacation through New Year's. She had no close relatives other than her parents, who at this very moment might be going about their appointed task of feeding starving children. Little did they know that their own daughter was hungry back home in the good old U.S.A. At the moment, her stomach was so empty that it was nibbling on her backbone.

Jake sighed in his sleep. She wouldn't wake him. The baby would do that soon enough.

Jake shifted position, and she almost spoke to him. Then, her cheeks burning, she was glad that she hadn't. She could feel his erection through her coat. It was pressed hard against her back, and there was absolutely no mistaking what it was.

He apparently wasn't aware that he was pushing against her, and she had no idea whether to move away, thereby waking him and probably embarrassing both of them, or if the proper thing to do under these circumstances was to lie still and feign sleep.

She feigned sleep. She regulated her breathing, trying to keep it even, willing her stomach not to make hungry noises, when all the while her heart was racing and her head was spinning. Not to mention the rest of her, which, heaven help her, was responding the way any healthy woman's body would respond to a sexual stimulus from a good-looking man.

He awoke with a start. Mariel squeezed her eyes shut and held her breath.

Taking the baby with him, he rolled away from Mariel and lay quietly as Jessica fussed herself awake. Mariel didn't move. She remained as if frozen until Jake began to prepare the last of the milk for the baby. Then she sat up and blinked her eyes, smiling with what she thought would pass for supreme innocence.

"Good morning," he grunted, more interested in Jessica than in her. That should have pleased Mariel, but instead she felt slighted.

"How about handing me a clean diaper?" he suggested.

Silently she got up and went to the stack of dry cotton rectangles, folded two together and presented them to him. He unpinned the diaper that Jessica was wearing, looking as if he were all thumbs.

"Those diapers look dry," he said, nodding toward the ledge where they hung. "You might as well fold them up and stuff them in my pack. The way this kid goes through these things, we're going to need them." He slid the clean diaper under the baby's buttocks and drew the fabric up between her legs, pinning the corners haphazardly, his brow furrowed in concentration.

Mariel fought the urge to smile at his awkwardness and did as he suggested. As she was withdrawing her hand from the pack, the apple rolled out. She held it up. "Did you say we could eat this for breakfast?" she asked.

Jake had finished his diapering chores and had begun the slow, laborious process of feeding the baby. Jessica was fretting because she couldn't get the milk fast enough; Jake was concentrating on speeding up the process. He spared Mariel a quick, impersonal glance. "Sure," he said. "My knife's in the pack, too."

Mariel sliced the apple into quarters. She held one out toward Jake, but his hands were full.

"Here," Mariel said, holding the apple to his lips. After a quick look at her, he bit from it, chewed, and swallowed. "There's more," said Mariel, and he opened his mouth, letting her pop the bit of apple into it.

"Thanks," he said.

"Want the other piece?" she said, waving it in front of him.

He eyed it briefly. "Maybe not. I'll save it for a few minutes, and that way it'll seem like I've eaten more than I really have."

"Suit yourself," Mariel said, but she ate her half of the apple all at once, savoring every last morsel. She was just as glad that she hadn't had to feed him the last part of the apple—it seemed too intimate by far for her to be putting food in his mouth. His lips had brushed her fingertips, and it had sent shivers through her, shivers that had nothing to do with the chill and damp of the cave. Maybe he had noticed it, too, since he hadn't wanted her to feed him the rest.

Mariel busied herself with cleaning the knife while Jake finished feeding Jessica. She felt the corduroy of her slacks and found they were still too damp to wear. She moved them closer to the fire, and Jake said, "Are my jeans dry yet?"

She felt them, unable to avoid a mind's-eye picture of Jake peeling them off last night. What was wrong with her? Why wasn't she handling this better? She shouldn't be unnerved by this man—she hardly knew him.

And then she thought about waking up with him, about his erection pressed against her, and she realized that she knew him, knew some things about him well, and that her awareness was normal. But it wasn't comfortable. That was the problem. It wasn't comfortable at all.

"Well, what about my jeans? Dry or not?" Jake demanded.

"Almost," she said, dropping the fabric as if it burned her hands.

Jake ate the last quarter of the apple and stood up abruptly, leaving the baby lying on his jacket, crowding Mariel in her space. She fled to the other end of the cave, keeping an eye on him as she put the knife back in his pack and, for something to do, rearranged the things in her tote bag.

Still facing away from her, Jake pulled on his jeans. She turned her head, her hair falling over her face, as he zipped the fly with a quick flip of the wrist.

After pulling on his socks and boots, Jake took the empty thermos lid outside, which gave Mariel the opportunity to compose herself before he came back with icicles to melt. By that time, Mariel was kneeling by the fire, holding Jessica in front of her like a shield.

Mariel murmured to the baby as Jake pulled a disposable razor out of his pack and began to shave. He had no mirror, but his strokes were swift and sure. He seemed quiet, thoughtful, perhaps even dour.

At first she didn't plan to speak to him, but she couldn't stand the silence. Finally, for the purpose of testing his mood, she observed, "You travel well prepared."

"Habit," he said. He poured water over the razor to rinse it, dried it on his jeans, and returned it to the pack.

"You always carry a backpack?"

"Only when I know I'm going to have to trek miles and miles through a winter storm," he said.

"Seriously," she said, trying to cajole him into the kind of banter that had made them both feel better earlier.

"Things happen. That's why I keep it in my truck. I work far from home sometimes, and I carry the stuff I'll need if I have to spend the night. That's all," he said. He looked at her, then looked away. She had the feeling that he was edgy about being cooped up here with her and the baby, with diapers hung up to dry, nothing but the rocky floor to sit on, and not enough to eat.

As if to verify her thoughts, he said gruffly, "I'm going outside for a minute."

The call of nature or merely a longing for fresh air and a bit of freedom? Mariel didn't know. She tried to think, which wasn't easy on an almost empty stomach. What she thought was that they had to get out of here. Not only for Jessica's sake, but also so that she and Jake wouldn't end up at each other's throats.

JAKE CRAWLED through the tunnel to the outside, toward fresh air. He'd felt cramped all of a sudden: he'd felt crowded. The atmosphere inside the cave was so worrisome and tense. Mariel was beautiful and unconsciously provocative. Had she known what it did to him when she allowed her fingers to touch his lips while she was feeding him that piece of apple? Hadn't she felt the electricity vibrating between them when their eyes met, when they spoke to each other?

Maybe she was too worried about their circumstances to notice. But he noticed, and that was why he'd put on still-damp jeans. He could no longer wear only his underwear around her without giving himself away, long jacket or no.

He emerged into the cold, still thinking about Mariel, when he suddenly realized the beauty of the scene before him. The ice storm had wrought a miracle. Icicles hung from every tree branch and from every projection on the cliff, glittering in the sun. Each individual needle of the surrounding evergreens was coated with ice, and it glimmered and shimmered brighter than the tinsel on a Christmas tree. On the ground, water ran in crystalline rivulets; the air was filled with the tinkle of ice as it fell from the trees.

He wanted Mariel to see it. He called her name, his voice filled with excitement.

As Mariel came out of the cave with Jessica in her arms, Jake held back the brambles and helped her get her footing. He watched her eyes widen as an expression of delight spread over her face.

"Oh, Jake, isn't it beautiful?" she murmured, her breath frosty in the air.

"Like a winter wonderland," he agreed in a hushed voice.

"Didn't I tell you about miracles?" she asked him.

"Miracles," he said staunchly, "had nothing to do with this. A winter ice storm, that's what did it. It could have happened on any night."

"But we found the baby last night, and now this," Mariel reminded him.

"And this morning we have nothing to eat. If someone were granting miracles, I think he'd leave us a box of granola, at the very least. Or maybe a few sticks of firewood, since we're getting low," he said wryly.

"Let's gather up our things and leave here as soon as we can," Mariel said.

"Too late," he said, gesturing at the clouds gathering behind the mountains in the distance. "Another storm is on the way."

"Another! But it can't be! We just had a storm," she said, though the clouds were all too visible, hunkering on the horizon.

"Just another one of those miracles of yours," Jake said with a sly look that Mariel ignored. "Besides," he said, "you should be happy to have a safe place to ride out this new storm. Remember yesterday? I don't think either of us wants to go through something like that again.''

"I'm sick of that cave. And Jessica needs something to eat. We can't stay here any longer. We've got to go."

Jake could see that Mariel was prepared to be stubborn about this, but he was no longer sure that there were houses around here.

"Go? No way. A few hours and the storm will have passed over," he said. He cocked his head and assessed the clouds with an experienced eye before sliding a comforting arm around Mariel's shoulders. "We'll be on our way by early afternoon," he said soothingly.

"What's Jessica going to eat? What are *we* going to eat?" she said, her inflection rising unnaturally at the end of each sentence. She didn't want Jake to notice, but she felt as if she were going to cry.

"We'll have water to drink," Jake said calmly.

"Water! Maybe we can survive for a while on water, but what about the baby? And we only have one stick of firewood left," Mariel reminded him, exasperated that he wouldn't see this her way.

"I was thinking that I'd walk along the face of the cliff and try to figure out where we should go when we leave here. I'll try to find some dry firewood then."

"Jake, let's make a run for it. We can outrun this storm, I know we can!"

"What if we can't? No, Mariel, we're staying where we are."

Mariel gazed down into Jessica's trusting eyes. How long could a baby Jessica's size go without food? She had to make Jake understand that they couldn't continue to stay in the cave.

"Jake," she said desperately, "can't you see? It's Jessica's life we're talking about. If she doesn't get something to eat soon—real baby formula, I mean—she'll get weaker and weaker, and she may die. We can't do this to her, Jake. We've got to leave. We've got to!''

"And what if we get stuck in a snowstorm, Mariel, the way we were caught in the ice storm last night? What about that? What if *we* die? Jessica has precious little chance of survival without us. Don't you realize that?'' He shook off Mariel's arm and disappeared into the cave, emerging in a few moments wearing his backpack.

Mariel's eyes stung with unshed tears. She turned her head away so that he wouldn't see.

"Go back in the cave and try to keep the fire going. I'm going to find some dry wood before the snow starts," Jake said. With that, he stalked away along the track, his boots crunching on fallen icicles and acorns.

Mariel stood stunned, the baby in her arms, her fear a metallic taste in her mouth. She was hungry. So hungry. And suddenly she felt very, very tired.

Jake had disappeared into the forest, and he hadn't even looked back.

Chapter Five

Mariel crawled blindly into the cave, scarcely able to think. But she *had* to think.

For one thing, she had to see if there was anything left from Jake's pack to feed Jessica, anything at all. Jake had been worried about the storm, but there was one thing they hadn't discussed. During their impassioned discussion of the coming storm, neither of them had mentioned that once the snow stopped, they might not be able to get out of here at all. They could be marooned for days.

The temperature in the cave was warm compared to that outside, so she pulled on her dry corduroys, slipped off her coat and zipped out the wool lining. She wrapped the baby in the coat lining and set her down beside the jumble of things that Jake had dumped out of his pack, hemming the baby in between the cave wall and her own tote bag so that she couldn't roll. Jessica suddenly became absorbed in studying her tiny fists, which was all to the good. It left Mariel free to explore Jake's belongings.

She set the empty thermos aside. Next, she inspected the waterproof canister of matches, and a camper's set of interlocked fork and spoon, which almost made her laugh. At the moment, it seemed to be the last thing they needed.

There was also a small roll of cash—also virtually useless unless they burned the bills to keep the fire going—a hammer, and a rope.

Great, Mariel said to herself, *just great.* He had left nothing that could be useful to her at that point.

Next she rummaged through her purse. In it was a roll of mints, unopened, and an overlooked package of crackers. Deep in the zippered side pocket she found a small packet of sugar.

These things promised some sustenance, but not much. How long until Jessica began crying with hunger? At least, with the ice storm of the night before and the approaching snowstorm, there would be no lack of water.

Mariel had to keep up her spirits or she'd go crazy. She'd taken another look at the scudding clouds overhead, and she knew that the snow would not hold off for long. The fire was rapidly dying; she hoped Jake would be back soon with dry firewood.

She picked up Jessica and held her in her arms, rocking her gently until she fell asleep. Then Mariel placed the bundle in the nest between her tote bag and the wall and crawled out of the cave. How long had Jake been gone? Half an hour? More?

As she stood in front of the opening, snowflakes began to sift from the sky, gently at first, then borne on a biting wind. Mariel's eyes searched for Jake's familiar red-and-black lumberjack jacket among the tree trunks, but she didn't see him.

She wrapped her arms around herself, too cold to stay outside and yet too worried to go back in the cave. Where was Jake? Why didn't he come back?

JAKE WAS HEADING into unknown country, all right. Without a map, with only the sun to give direction, he didn't know if he would run smack into a river, rough terrain or a road. After he stubbed his toe against an upturned stump, he kept his eyes on the ground and wished he were at home watching TV, his feet propped on his favorite footstool.

Adventures like this were tailor-made for television. They did not happen to real people. He shouldn't be following a winding trail through the woods, trying to keep the direction of the cave in his mind while his stomach complained that it hadn't been fed lately. He wondered how long he'd be able to keep up his strength if he didn't get something to eat soon.

There were deer in these woods. And rabbits; he knew that from his disastrous experience yesterday, when he'd tried to brake for one. Jake wasn't a hunter, and he knew nothing about trapping. His survival skills did not include converting live animals into food. Still, if it came down to feeding Mariel...

Mariel. He said her name out loud, there in the silent forest. He liked to say her name.

He shouldn't be thinking about her. One of the benefits of having to gather firewood was that he was able to get away from her.

He needed to figure out what to do. This morning, when he'd awakened, it would have been so easy—and so stupid—to reach for her lush curves and fit himself to them. Warming the baby between them had been his idea, and it was for the baby's benefit. But it was also supposed to serve the purpose of keeping him away from Mariel. It hadn't worked.

Those last few dark hours before light, during the second time they'd huddled on the cave floor trying to

stay warm, he'd hardly slept at all. Mariel had; her
breathing had been slow and even. That was good.
What wasn't good was that he had lain awake, thinking about the tantalizing smoothness of her skin, the
creaminess of her breasts, so inadequately concealed by
that wisp of a bra, and the curve of her waist, flowing
so delectably into the roundness of her hips.

He'd only met her yesterday. What would she think
about a man who was supposed to be getting them out
of this mess but could hardly think of anything except
the details of her body and how longingly he wished to
abandon himself to their exploration?

When they had slept together the first time, his hands
on her rib cage, her heart fluttering beneath them, it had
taken a supreme act of will not to slide his hands upward and under that lacy bra to cup her lush round
breasts. He already knew how they'd lie heavily in his
hands, how they'd taste sweet to his lips. He had wanted
to nuzzle beneath the soft trailing hair on her neck and
nibble gently at the fragrant skin there, his breath teasing her ear. He had wanted to hear the soft whisper of
her skin against his as she turned within the circle of his
arms until the two of them rested front to front, lips
together.

He could imagine brushing aside those bikini panties
and seeking the silken wet center of her, making her
quiver with desire. She would reach around him and
pull his hips toward hers, her fingernails cutting into his
flesh as she felt him surging against her. He would begin to move, and she would, too, and then—no. He
couldn't think about it. He *wouldn't*. If he did, he'd
march back into the cave and—What was that quaint
expression? Oh, yes, he'd have his way with Mariel.

A dream. All of it. A fantasy that had nothing to do with reality. The reality was that they had to stay alive and find their way out of here after the snowstorm had passed.

Jake looked around, trying to determine his location. The mountain directly above looked like the peak that was known, for some unfathomable reason, as Old Barker. This was a rural area, thinly populated, and the interstate highway that Mariel had been looking for was miles away. He had no idea how to get out of these woods.

The track he was on wound through the dense forest; he saw where a lumber cut had been made through the trees. He jogged along it, and eventually he saw what he was looking for: a tall tree with branches placed so that he could climb it.

He jumped up and gained a grip on a lower branch, sending a thin coating of ice tinkling down the trunk. Then he swung up his legs and pulled himself onto a sturdier branch, dislodging even more ice. He continued upward until he had a fairly good view of his surroundings.

He glanced back in the direction from which he'd come. He saw the cliff and tried to pick out the entrance to the cave, which would be difficult, because it was so small. He detected movement, and that was when he saw the tiny figure in the tan all-weather coat, its drabness broken by a red scarf blowing in the wind. *Mariel,* he thought, a thrill of pleasure rippling through him. He wanted to wave, to shout, but he thought it might frighten her.

Mariel looked no bigger than an insect from this vantage point. Suddenly Jake was afraid she was planning to strike out on her own in the snowstorm. The thought terrified him. She wouldn't do that. Or would she? She was a woman who was accustomed to making her own decisions, after all. Why should she listen to him? He watched the figure that was Mariel, but it didn't move.

He didn't want to take his eyes from her, for fear that she'd disappear, but he couldn't stay there forever. Telling himself that she'd have more sense than to move on alone, he tore his eyes away from the Mariel-figure and scanned the opposite direction. He was looking for a puff of smoke that would indicate a chimney, a driveway that led to a house, a road, a movement, *anything.* All he saw was bare-branched trees, their trunks dark with melting ice.

Then he saw something that wasn't a tree. Neither did it seem to be a house. At first he thought it was part of a distant mountain, but then he looked again. It was...a tower?

He eased himself upward to the next branch for a better view. It was *probably* a tower, he decided, and it seemed to be constructed of gray stone.

His precarious position in the tree afforded him only a glimpse of it. But at least it gave him hope that there was help ahead. That, for the moment, was enough.

He glanced back at the place where he'd seen Mariel, but she was gone. She'd disappeared. Had she gone back into the cave, or had she left?

He made haste down the tree trunk, stopping to snatch a bit of mistletoe from one of the branches and shove in into his coat's breast pocket. He thought it might amuse Mariel. He had to keep thinking that she'd be there.

MARIEL'S TEETH were chattering from the cold. Or maybe it was fear. She knew that Jake wasn't coming back.

Was she afraid for him? No, she was afraid for all of them. They would die out here. It was Christmas Eve day, and they were going to die.

Jake must have decided that he would go on without her and the baby; certainly it would be easier for him not to have a woman and a child to drag along. So he had walked out into the face of a blizzard. They had argued, and he had been so angry that he'd left.

She looked at Jessica, so pink and sweet, sleeping as if she hadn't a worry in the world. *Poor little thing,* Mariel thought. *Abandoned in the woods, and now this.*

Mariel gathered a few twigs and pieces of bark from the place where the firewood had been stacked, and she found another log in the far corner of the cave. She noticed with some surprise a previously undetected crevice from which dank air seeped, but she didn't want to waste the precious flashlight battery to investigate what it was.

She tossed the bark on the fire, knowing that it wouldn't keep the flame going for long. But she did want to boil the water in the thermos lid for Jessica. At least she could offer the baby that.

She huddled at the edge of the fire, listening and waiting. Waiting and listening. And still there was no sign of Jake.

ON HIS WAY BACK to the cave, Jake found a good-size fallen tree and rolled it over to expose the dry wood. Using his trusty hatchet, he managed to split off several reasonably dry, seasoned logs.

There was an ominous feeling in the air as he started back to the cave, the firewood in his arms, and he kept his eyes on the encroaching clouds, knowing that if they obscured the sun he'd be in trouble. The sun was his only directional guide. He hadn't taken time to notch the trees as he walked, so he might wander off the track if snow fell hard enough to obscure his vision.

He should feel more successful than he did. He was returning with wood that would burn, wood that would keep them warm until after the snow fell. They would be snug in their cave.

But he, too, was worried about how long the baby could survive without food. As he trudged through the woods, unbidden pictures flooded his brain, freeze-frame images that made him quicken his step. He thought about Mariel carrying the baby through snowdrifts, unable to see in the whited-out landscape. He thought about them falling down, and Mariel unable to get up again, and the baby crying until suddenly the crying stopped.

He was angry with himself for not having made things clear before he left. He should have extracted a promise from Mariel that she wouldn't take the baby and leave. Why hadn't he taken that precaution? Why had he been so rash and bullheaded?

Snow began to fall. *If Mariel and Jessica are still in the cave, I'll never get drunk again,* he promised himself, though it wasn't much of a promise. He hadn't been drunk since a buddy's bachelor party five years ago.

If Mariel and Jessica are still in the cave, I'll never argue with her again, he decided. The whole exercise reeked of "Step on a crack, you'll break your mother's back, step on a line, you'll break your mother's spine,'' childish doggerel that had stuck with him to this day.

If Mariel is still there, I'll pull her into my arms and kiss her was Jake's final offering. And that was one promise that he fully intended to keep.

JESSICA BEGAN TO SQUALL, and Mariel, giving up on the eyedropper, used the spoon from Jake's pack to ladle sugar water into her mouth. It kept her quiet while Mariel tried to think.

If Jake didn't come back, she would wait until the storm passed and then dig her way out of the cave. Then she and Jessica would head toward her car.

Not that it would be easy, with snowdrifts covering the road. Considering the fact that they seemed to be in a completely deserted part of the world, she could hardly expect a snowplow to come through and clear it.

After she'd swallowed most of the sugar water, Jessica was due for a diaper change, which Mariel was able to accomplish more easily now that she'd gained experience. She rocked Jessica until she fell asleep and laid her in the nest she'd made from the lining of her coat.

Mariel felt cold; without its lining, her coat wasn't particularly warm. She crept closer to the fire, which was now reduced to a bed of glowing coals.

For lack of anything else to do, she used a bit of precious light from the flashlight and went to look for a scrap of bark, or a bit of paper, or anything else that would burn. And then she saw the log.

There couldn't be another log there. It was impossible. Jake himself had said they'd used the last piece of wood earlier, and Mariel had figured that the log she'd found a while ago, a spindly, meager log, had simply been overlooked. But here was another.

It felt strange to be picking up the log and putting it on the fire, and she wondered how she could have missed it earlier. Then she felt a blast of cool air from the cave entrance and went to check on the weather.

When Mariel emerged from the cave, snowflakes were drifting down in clumps, almost covering the ground. The sky was the shade that her mother had always called tattletale gray, only this sky was telling no tales. Neither were the trees. She saw no sign of Jake.

She thought she had prepared herself never to see him again, but now that she knew that there was virtually no hope he'd return, her heart sank to the pit of her stomach and settled there like a rock.

Well, she couldn't blame him for trying to get out of here. She had no doubt that he'd send someone to rescue her and the baby. In fact, that might have been his purpose in leaving. Now she could only hope that he'd find help—and find it fast. But who could get through in the face of the second major storm in twenty-four hours? Only Santa Claus, she thought, trying to feel lighthearted. Santa Claus and his airborne reindeer, soaring through the sky.

Jake would laugh at her. She was almost laughing at herself. But what if Jake didn't get through to someplace where there were people? What if he was in worse shape than she and the baby were, lost somewhere in these vast, uninhabited woods?

She wouldn't think about that. No point in dwelling on the problems. Time to get on with business. Time to think about how they were going to make it through the rest of the day, and probably longer, without food.

But when she went back in the cave and saw Jessica sleeping so peacefully, it was Mariel's undoing. She didn't mind all of this so much for herself. After all, she was a grown woman, thirty years old, and had experienced some of what life had to offer.

But Jessica was a baby. An infant. She wasn't even old enough to creep or crawl, and she couldn't hold her head up to see what the world was about. She'd never had a chance, and if they died in this awful cave, she never would.

Mariel buried her face in her hands. It was so unfair. So, so unfair...

JAKE STRUGGLED toward the cave, seeing no sign of Mariel. The snow was falling so heavily now that there was no way he would have been able to detect her departing footprints even if they were there.

Then he was at the entrance of the cave, dropping pieces of wood in his eagerness to see within. It was silent inside, a forbidding sign. If Mariel and the baby were in there, the baby would be hungry and she would be crying. Or Mariel would be talking to the baby and he would be able to hear her as he made his way through the opening.

He pressed through the brambles and crawled through the tunnellike entrance. And then, as his eyes adjusted to the gloom of the cave, he saw the flames and the hunched-over shape beside them.

Jake fell into the cave, firewood scattering in every direction.

"Mariel!" he cried, unable to believe that she was there. She was really there. He had talked himself into believing that she was headstrong enough to leave.

The figure rose as he staggered to his feet. "Jake! Oh, Jake!" she said, and the fire was bright enough for him to see the tears drying in salty streaks on her cheeks.

Then, with no warning, she was catapulting into his arms, laughing and sobbing at the same time. She flung her arms around his neck, unmindful of the snow clumped on the shoulders of his coat, and pressed her body tightly against his. His heart began to throb so strongly that he thought it would burst out of his chest.

"I thought you had gone," she said, sobbing into the front of his jacket. "I thought you had left us."

"I wouldn't," he said, wrapping his arms solidly around her and drawing in her warmth. Her sweater was soft, her body voluptuous, her hair tickling his mouth. He moved his head slightly, only to precipitate the uplifting of her face to his. Her eyes were silvery blue, the pupils defined by rims of a darker hue. They were shining with happiness.

"I thought you might be planning to send someone to rescue us," she said in a choked voice.

"I was sure you'd left. I saw you standing outside the entrance of the cave earlier, and I figured you had waited until I was out of sight and had taken the baby, looking for a safer place. When I thought that, I was so scared—"

"You? Scared? I don't believe it," she said, her eyes searching his face.

He enfolded her more tightly in his arms. He could feel her heartbeat, see the pulse of it at her temple. All at once he knew that he would sacrifice his life for her or the baby if need be. He had read about people who did things like that, but before, from his limited perspective, that altruistic mind-set had meant nothing to him. He certainly hadn't thought he would ever feel that way about anyone himself.

"I—I made all kinds of promises to myself while I was on my way back with the wood and thinking you wouldn't be here," he said unevenly.

"Like what?" Her voice was almost a whisper.

"Like—*this*," he whispered back, bending his head over hers.

Her fingers fluttered at the back of his neck and were still. He fitted his lips to hers, so perfectly, so beautifully, and slid one hand up her spine to weave it into the loose curls hanging below her shoulders.

She sighed, her breath gentle against his cheek, and drew his head down even farther. He deepened the kiss as her mouth opened to his, the textures of her lips and teeth and tongue a powerful aphrodisiac. They were instantly lost in the moment, clinging to each other, pouring themselves into the connection between them. Jake forgot his physical hunger and gave in to a more elemental one, wanting to feast, but not on food. In that moment he realized that she wanted him as much as he wanted her, and he was so wildly happy at the thought that all he wanted to do was to follow his instincts, which would take them both into realms that he had so far only imagined.

She slid her hands into his coat, her fingers finding their way, moving under his shirt, searching for warm skin. He felt as if he were floating in a warm dark world where normal rules didn't apply and where pleasure was the only sensation. He felt her knees buckle and wrapped his arms around her to lower her to the sand.

And then the baby cried.

It took a moment for the noise to register. Time and place seeped back into their consciousnesses; they remembered. The storm. The cave. The baby.

Jake was the first to speak. "Is she all right?" he asked.

Mariel only breathed deeply, a kind of gasp, and then she righted herself. Her hands dropped to her sides, and she closed her eyes for a moment as if to clear her head.

And in that moment, Jake saw that it was regrettably inappropriate in this time and in this place to think that they could relate to each other in any way that didn't ensure their survival and the baby's. While making love might make them feel gloriously and completely alive, it wouldn't solve their problems. It would only make them go away temporarily.

"The noise woke her," Mariel said, sounding like her ordinary self as she backed away, smoothing her hair self-consciously. In a few seconds, she was kneeling in front of Jessica, murmuring sweet nothings in that solicitous voice she always used with the baby and ignoring Jake completely.

Jake waited until his body returned to normal and then bent and retrieved the firewood. Mariel, he had discovered, had a strong motherly instinct. Yet he couldn't help feeling disappointed; he wanted to hold her in his arms, to whisper fiercely that he would never let anything harm her, that he would give his life for her if need be.

But he couldn't do anything of the sort. Mariel was changing the baby's diaper. The storm was roaring outside the cave. Jake made himself wedge a few sticks of firewood on the fire and deposited the rest where the old woodpile had been.

"You know, after you left I found another stick of firewood. And then, just a while ago, another," Mariel said, lifting her head. Apparently she had chosen to act as if nothing had passed between them. Well, he didn't know any better way to handle it, and two could play that game.

"That's impossible. I put the last stick on the fire this morning before I went out looking for wood."

Mariel didn't notice his reluctance to pursue the topic. She went on talking, her hands busy with the baby. "It was strange, and I thought I must have overlooked those two logs this morning," she said.

He detected an unnatural brightness in her tone. She *had* been affected by what had happened between them. The thought gave him hope.

But at that moment he couldn't ignore what she was saying, because it was, he knew, bald fantasy. "Mariel, Mariel..." he said gently, genuinely concerned about her. What was this? Was her mind playing tricks on her?

"Well, it happened," she said flatly.

"It *is* Christmas," he said, hoping to gloss over this disturbing development. He *knew* there had been no other logs this morning. There was no doubt in his mind.

She shook her head and laughed. He was relieved to see the corners of her mouth tilting upward, even though it reminded him that he could still taste her on his lips.

Mariel, quietly efficient, had bundled the baby into her arms and was swaying back and forth, murmuring endearments.

Jake removed his coat and spread it on the sand. "Time for a diaper change?" he asked.

Mariel shook her head. "Not yet."

"Then we might as well both sit on my coat. This storm may take its own sweet time in passing."

Jessica fussed and fretted until at last she dropped off to sleep. "I scraped up a package of mints and another package of crackers while you were gone," Mariel told him. "And I fed Jessica sugar water."

"She seems okay."

Mariel studied the baby's face, a frown bisecting her forehead. "I think so."

Jake made himself concentrate on other things besides Mariel's closeness. He didn't want her to see how worried he was, so he stood up and began to pace back and forth at the back of the cave. He still couldn't believe her claim that she'd found two more pieces of wood after he left. He kept glancing at her out of the corner of his eye, searching for some sign that she was becoming mentally unstable. She seemed completely normal. And sexy, though he didn't think she realized it.

"How's our flashlight doing?" he made himself ask.

"Almost gone," Mariel said.

He reached down and switched it on, mostly for the hell of it. The circle of its beam was orange and dim.

"Oh, by the way, I found a fissure of some kind in the wall," Mariel said.

"No kidding! It can't be very big," he said, unable to square what she was saying with what he knew to be true. He had thoroughly vetted the cave last night. He hadn't seen any fissure.

"I think we didn't notice it before because it's way at the back of the cave and could have been partly obscured by the woodpile," she said.

Jake, with marked reluctance, took a look. He couldn't believe his eyes when he saw it. Sure enough, there was a crack in the rock.

"Why, there is something here!" he exclaimed.

"Did you think I made it up?"

"I don't know what to think anymore." He saw that the fissure was barely wide enough for him to slip his arm through, and he didn't know what made him do it, but he reached into the crack. As his hand groped within the dark space, his fingers closed around a cylindrical shape. Cautiously he withdrew it, then stared at the object in his hand. Then he reached back in and pulled out two more cans, scarcely able to believe his eyes.

"What are you doing?" Mariel asked. He was blocking her view.

"Bringing home the bacon," Jake replied, in a choked voice as he turned to show her a can of Vienna sausage, a can of date-nut bread, and a can of evaporated milk.

Chapter Six

"Where did those come from?" Mariel asked in sheer disbelief.

He nodded his head toward the crevice. "They were in there."

"Why?" she asked, turning the can of milk over and over in her hands. It was exactly what they needed, and she could hardly believe that it had been there all the time.

"I don't know *why*, Mariel. Can't we simply be grateful that it *was?*" he said, sitting down beside her. He could no longer think there was anything wrong with Mariel's mental faculties, not when everything she'd said had turned out to be true. He was beginning to wonder if his own mind was playing tricks on him instead.

"The milk has to be diluted for drinking. We can mix it with melted snow. It should get Jessica through the rest of the day, at least," Mariel said with a kind of awe.

"The other stuff is for us," he said. "I hope you like Vienna sausages."

Mariel wrinkled her nose. "Under normal circumstances, I wouldn't touch them. But I'm hungry. Very hungry," she added.

"And the date-nut bread," he said. "Actually, I've always liked it, especially when it's spread with cream cheese."

"Did you try sticking your hand further into the crevice? You might find some," Mariel said impishly, and he laughed.

They ate ravenously, and when Jessica woke up, they were ready with milk, which they had mixed with an equal amount of water. The baby was greedy, rooting for the eyedropper and fussing each time Mariel refilled it. Feeding her was a tedious job.

The feeding accomplished, Jake took Jessica from Mariel and balanced the infant on his upraised knees. "Too bad babies don't come with blueprints to tell us what's where and how it works," he said.

"Or instruction books."

"Or user's manuals."

"Do you think we're doing everything right?" Mariel asked anxiously.

"I don't know," Jake said. "But doesn't she seem okay? She's smiling. Look."

"She is! Well, I think she likes us," Mariel said.

"I know she does. By the way, what's the status of the storm?"

Mariel sat down beside him. "Still raging."

"We need to plan what to do when we leave here," Jake said, becoming so serious that Mariel didn't speak but waited for him to continue.

He told her quickly about the tower he thought he had seen when he climbed the tree, and he suggested that they head in that direction when they left the cave.

"Was there any smoke near this tower? Any sign of life?" Mariel wanted to know.

Jake shook his head. "Not that I could tell."

"How about in any other direction?"

"Nothing at all."

"Jake, where *are* we? You're from around here. You should have some idea."

"We're lost, but we're going to get out of here today. I promise you that," he said with an air of determination.

Her eyes were troubled, and Jake reached out and enclosed her hand in his. "I promise," he repeated in a firm voice, and because he sounded so sure, she was, too.

THE SNOW STOPPED before the hour was out, and, fortified by their meager lunch of Vienna sausage, they set out.

With Jake leading the way, they waded through the freshly fallen snow, breaking a trail. Jake carried the baby inside his coat, and Jessica peeped out in round-eyed astonishment.

Mariel smiled at Jessica, thinking what a cute baby she was. Then she laughed at Jake.

"What's wrong?" he asked.

"You look so funny," she said, still grinning. "You look pregnant, carrying her in front of you like that."

"I kind of wondered what pregnancy would be like," he told her, and she laughed.

"How do you like it?"

He made a face. "It's tolerable," he drawled, which only made her laugh again.

"You should stop laughing and talking so much," he said sternly. "You'll get exhausted again."

"Oh," she said, feeling liberated by the sun peeping out from behind the clouds, and the bright snow, and the sky, washed as blue as bottle glass. "Let me enjoy

this. After all that time in the cave, I feel as if I can
breathe again. I want to dance and sing and play the
way I did when I was a child!'' She bounded through
the snow until she was walking backward in front of
him, her eyes sparkling.

''You can dance and sing if you want,'' he said, trying to keep a straight face, ''but I can't. I'm pregnant.''

She laughed merrily, the sound reminding him of silver bells.

She looked so beautiful, so carefree, so different from
the way she had looked in the cave. At the moment, all
he wanted to do was to pull her into his arms and kiss
her.

She threw out her arms, as if to embrace everything,
and he thought he had never seen anything as beautiful
as Mariel welcoming herself back to the world after an
ordeal that both of them had thought might be the end
of them.

Then she skipped back to him and took his hand.
''I'll behave now. I wanted to get all that out of my
system, that's all,'' she said with uncharacteristic
meekness. He wondered if she knew that even the presence of her hand in his aroused him, then decided she
didn't. If she knew, she wouldn't do it so casually.

He decided to stick to business. ''Mariel, it's not a
matter of behavior. It's a matter of conserving your energy in case of a problem,'' he said.

''You mean, in case that tower you saw was a mi-
rage?''

''I don't *think* it was, but I didn't *think* there was
firewood left in the cave, and then there were two more
pieces. The things I take for granted don't seem to be

true anymore, and things that I thought weren't there, including the food I found in the cave, *were*," he said.

"Magic," Mariel said. "It's Christmastime, you know."

He didn't answer, and they walked on quietly for a few more steps until Mariel realized that Jake wasn't going to rise to the bait. She decided to try a new tact.

"I wonder what it's really like to be pregnant. I don't mean just carrying a baby inside your coat," she ventured.

"It's not as if I would know," Jake pointed out.

"I think it must make a woman feel special to be pregnant."

"I think it must make her feel fat," he said in all honesty.

"A baby is not classified as fat," Mariel said indignantly.

"Did you hear that?" he said into the front of his coat. "A baby is not classified as fat."

"Wah," said Jessica.

"Oh, my gosh, did you hear that? She said something!" he shouted.

"All she did was get her vocal cords into gear while she was yawning. It doesn't mean anything."

"Knowing what I now know about babies, it probably means 'Change my diaper,'" Jake said, with more than a touch of irony.

"We only have one clean diaper left."

"If you're still in the wish-making business, you should wish for a box of Flubbies, or whatever they call those disposable things babies wear."

Mariel dissolved into laughter. "They're not called Flubbies, but that's close enough."

"I'd hate to turn her over to her parents with a full-fledged case of diaper rash."

"I don't think she has any parents," Mariel told him seriously.

"Of course she does."

"Well, they're not anywhere around."

"She didn't appear out of thin air. She had to come from somewhere."

"Do you suppose she was left in the woods by a stork who was reluctant to risk dropping her down someone's chimney at this time of year?" Mariel asked innocently.

"Well, according to you, chimneys have been preempted by a VIP who has unorthodox ways of gaining entry into people's houses, so what's a stork to do? Look, Mariel," Jake said earnestly, "maybe this baby is the answer to your question. You know, the one we were discussing last night. How does a single woman get a child? We thought we'd covered all the possibilities, but there was one we didn't think about—finding one in the woods in the middle of an ice storm."

She favored him with a keen look to see if he was teasing her, but he stepped up his pace, and the snow was drifted high on this part of the trail, so she had to struggle to keep up.

The glare of the sun on snow was beginning to make Mariel's eyes ache when Jake suddenly stopped walking. "I see something!" he called excitedly over his shoulder.

"A house?"

"I'm not sure if it's a house, but I think it's what I saw earlier."

Mariel plunged through the snow and came to a halt behind him, looking over his shoulder at the tower.

It was visible through the treetops, a high, round gray stone structure rearing up against a bright blue sky. Pale yellow sunlight played over the walls, glittering on the snow frosting clinging to the spaces between the stones. Mariel caught her breath.

"It's a *castle*," she said, dazzled by the sight.

Jake drew her close by slipping an arm around her shoulders, something that she welcomed. She wondered if there was a chance that he would kiss her again, then decided that there wasn't. He had been acting matter-of-fact ever since they left the cave, and in spite of his teasing and their banter earlier, he didn't seem to recapture the highly charged feelings that they'd shared when they kissed. The realization left her with a mounting sense of disappointment.

"It's a castle, all right, unless we're both seeing things," he said.

"But what's it doing here? Where are we?" Mariel asked.

He squeezed her shoulder. "I don't know, but it's shelter. Come on," he said, taking her hand again.

They walked as fast as they could into the very heart of the woods. The track twisted and turned, sometimes doubling back upon itself, so that occasionally the tower was over Mariel's right shoulder, occasionally her left.

And then they came around a curve, and a clearing opened up in front of them. The castle was cupped in a hollow, as if within the palm of a hand. For a brief moment, birdsong trilled through the air, stopping suddenly and leaving them in pristine silence with nothing but the castle to fill their gaze.

The castle was complete with gatehouse towers reaching toward heaven, a huge, nail-studded oaken door, and a sagging drawbridge leading across a twenty-foot-wide moat. Speechless, Mariel and Jake stood and stared.

It looked like something out of a fairy tale. Somehow they expected people or horses to burst through the gate and run across the decrepit drawbridge, welcoming them with a fanfare of trumpets. But nothing like that happened. They saw no one, and they heard nothing but their own breathing.

And then Mariel saw the candle flickering in the gatehouse tower window. "Look."

"Someone's here."

"The candle is guiding us to shelter," Mariel said with certainty.

"If you say so," Jake said doubtfully.

"It's a Christmas custom in some countries to light a candle to guide travelers to a safe place," Mariel said in a rush. "They think that Christ wanders in the guise of a stranger to test the hospitality of people along the way. At Christmas, no one is turned away."

"I'm certainly glad to hear that," Jake said with great deliberation.

"You don't think much of the story, do you?" she challenged.

"At the moment, all I think is that I'm as hungry as a beast. Do we stand out here in the cold, or do we go in and— What did you say? Test their hospitality?"

Mariel knew that, inside, he was laughing at her. She kept her eyes on the candle flame. "We go in," she said, leading the way.

She hesitated at the start of the drawbridge. It was covered with snow, so they couldn't see the actual boards underneath.

"Do you think this bridge is safe?" she asked dubiously.

"You can hold the baby, and I'll go first." Jake prepared to divest himself of Jessica, but her loud wail rent the air.

"Better not," he said hastily, tucking Jessica into the front of his jacket again.

"I'll go first," Mariel decided, but in Jake's mind, the welcoming horses had become stallions intent on trampling to death anyone who got in their way, and the hounds a yapping horde, sure to tear her to pieces.

"We'll all go together," Jake said, and, mindful of every creak, they made their way across the drawbridge until they stood in the walled outer ward in front of the gatehouse.

It was three stories high, with two elongated twin towers connected by a roofed-over passageway. The top of the walls was crenellated, giving the effect of a giant set of teeth with every other tooth missing. The spaces between the crenellations were banked with snow.

A smaller door had been cut in the massive nail-studded oak door, and a rusty gong to their right presumably notified the occupants that they had visitors.

"Shall I ring it?" Mariel wanted to know.

"Let 'er rip," Jake answered. She picked up the waiting mallet and gave the gong a hard whack, sending a flock of birds fluttering off the battlements in panic.

"I don't think anyone's coming," Jake said after a few minutes had passed.

Mariel walked back to the edge of the drawbridge and looked up at the gatehouse window. "The candle is gone!" she exclaimed.

"Maybe they got a look at us and decided they didn't want to lodge such a scruffy-looking group," Jake said ruefully.

"I don't think that's it. The flame must have blown out."

"Well, do we stay here or go on?" Jake asked, shifting Jessica's weight impatiently.

"We're not in a position to leave. We have to feed Jessica," Mariel said. "We have to go in, whether anyone is here or not."

"Try the door. Maybe it's open."

Mariel pushed at the smaller door within the apparently immovable larger one, and was surprised when it swung open with little effort.

"After you," Jake said, standing back, and so Mariel went in first.

Once inside, she was overcome by the aura of the place; there was a haze of unreality about the castle. Mariel paused for a moment, glancing at Jake to see if he felt what she did, this kind of heightened awareness, as if she were breathing rarefied air.

Jake looked as if nothing were amiss, and so she shook off whatever imaginary effect she thought she'd felt and took notice of their surroundings.

They stood in a passage between the two towers of the gatehouse. Mariel saw a staircase leading up, but it was in deplorable condition, and she didn't see how anyone could have gotten upstairs to light the candle.

Puzzled, she stood on tiptoe to peer through a window in search of an inside stairway, but all she saw was the remnants of one, its boards strewn around the floor. While she was still wondering how anyone could have reached the upper story of the gatehouse with the staircases missing, she was startled to see two long ears waggling at her.

"There's something in here!" she said, turning to Jake.

Jake cocked his head to one side. "Animal? Vegetable? Mineral?"

"Animal, but I can't see *what,*" Mariel said as she continued through the passage to the castle courtyard, where she saw a doorway into the first floor of the gatehouse.

The actual door was missing. They could see directly inside. On a pile of straw, backed into a corner, was a goat.

"Bleah-h-h," went the goat.

"That's exactly the way I feel," Jake said in a conversational tone.

"Why, she's scared to death," Mariel said in concern. She didn't know how to behave around a goat; she'd never, as far as she could remember, met one before. She did, however, know that this goat was female, because of her large, swollen udder. The goat was gray and white, with great golden eyes, which were presently rolling around in their sockets to express extreme agitation.

"She's tame," Jake said.

"She probably belongs to the people who live here," she said, looking around for food or water and seeing none.

"Let's go find them." Jake couldn't wait to get to a warm place, where he could relax on a deeply cushioned chair and use the telephone.

Reluctantly Mariel followed him into the castle courtyard. The goat trailed after them, bleating all the while.

They were much too awed by the castle to pay attention to the goat. The courtyard was wide, and snow had drifted into all the corners. There was no sign of any inhabitants.

Mariel sized up her surroundings and determined that this one was small as castles went, with the inner courtyard about the size of two basketball courts. On their left were lean-tos built against the wall; to their right, more of the same.

"The bakehouse," Mariel said as they passed one door. A section of a thatch-roofed building elicited the comment. "That's the stable."

Jake couldn't resist asking, "How do you know?"

"I deal in legends. Legends take place in castles. I took college courses in medieval studies."

"I'm not so much interested in what's what as I am in where the people live."

Mariel pointed to a larger door directly ahead. "I'm sure that's the great hall. That's where people eat and spend leisure time. We should try there first."

Jake followed Mariel's lead, noting the stained-glass windows adorning the small enclosure to their right.

"That must be the chapel," he said. His brilliant deduction should show her that he knew something about medieval castles, too, but Mariel was forging ahead of him, leaving small, neat footprints in the snow.

"I don't see a doorbell," Mariel said as she stood in front of the door, and Jake had to laugh at the perplexed expression on her face.

"A doorbell? In a medieval castle?"

"Modern people must live here. You'd think there would be modern conveniences."

Jake shook his head. "No mod cons in this place. I don't see any telephone poles, or wires, or signs of any connection with the outside world."

Mariel's face fell, but only fleetingly. "All I hope is that they have a bathtub and water," she said firmly.

Jake knocked on the door, and the sound resounded hollowly within. No one answered. He knocked again, trying not to notice Mariel's look of discouragement.

Finally he said, "There's no one here."

She stared at him. "This big castle, stuck way out in the middle of the forest, and there's no one home? Why would anyone go to the trouble to put it here?" she asked in exasperation.

Jake looked at the blanket of snow, and at the icicles as long and as thick as his forearm hanging from the roofs of the nearby buildings. "I bet they've gone to Florida for the winter. I know *I* would," he said gloomily.

Without saying one more thing, Mariel marched around the courtyard, trying the locked chapel door, poking in corners, and jumping up to peer in windows, which were narrow and few. Jake followed her, being patient and consoling Jessica, whose diaper had reached the saturation point.

"You'll have to break in," Mariel said, looking panicky, when Jake reluctantly told her about the sorry state of Jessica's diaper.

"Bleah-h-h," went the goat.

"At least you didn't suggest that I go down the chimney," Jake said, but Mariel only wrinkled her nose at him.

"Anyway," he said, "this place belongs to someone who might not take kindly to breaking and entering, so maybe it's not a good idea."

"But this is an emergency," Mariel insisted. "Whoever lives here wouldn't want us to stay out in the freezing cold with a baby whose diaper is approaching flood status."

To emphasize her point, Jessica made a sound that was something like "glug."

"Okay, we'll take a look at the door to the great hall," he said.

Mariel found it difficult to keep up with Jake as he strode across the courtyard. The goat cavorted in their wake, something urgent in its manner. Mariel had no time to think about the goat; she was far more concerned about what they would do if they couldn't get inside the castle. Camp in the courtyard? Bed down in the gatehouse? Neither option seemed any more desirable than spending the night in a cave.

Jake studied the heavy door, and in a moment, using nothing more than a hammer and a Swiss army knife, he was pushing the door open. They stomped the thickly caked snow off their boots before Mariel followed Jake inside.

Once she was standing inside the great hall, Mariel realized that no one could be living there. It was long and dreary, dark and musty. The ceiling was vaulted in stone, and occupying one end of the room was a massive fireplace big enough to roast an ox. A dais at the other end held a long table with smaller tables arrayed below it, and a pale winter sun picked out the details of the faded tapestries on the walls.

"It's cold in here" was the first thing Jake said, his voice echoing back from the high ceiling.

Mariel, amazed at the authenticity of the place, was studying the elaborate tapestries. They were embroidered in warm browns and reds, with occasional flashes of yellow and blue here and there. The panels depicted stories—a hunt, the arrival of noblemen amid waving banners, knights jousting.

Jake's spirits were sinking. He might as well scrap the idea of a soft chair and a television set. The most modern convenience he saw was a packet of matches tossed carelessly on the hearth.

"Hello?" called Mariel, thinking she'd better make their presence known, in the unlikely event that someone was around. When no one answered, she looked at Jake and shrugged her shoulders.

"It's not much," Jake said with an audible sigh, "but we call it home. Let's take a look to make sure there aren't any more goats wandering around and to see if there's anything to eat." He took off at a fast clip for the far end of the hall.

"If this is like most castles, we won't find a kitchen. They always put the cookhouse far away from the hall and its apartments because of the danger of fire," Mariel was saying as Jake led the way into the room behind the dais, but she stopped and breathed, "Ooh," when she saw what was there.

"A kitchen," Jake said in an unbelieving voice. "An honest-to-goodness, real-life kitchen."

"With a stove," Mariel said. "And a refrigerator!" Things were looking up.

And in a matter of seconds, she was looking up—at Jake. He wrapped his arms around her, pulling her close.

"We're going to be all right, Mariel. We'll manage here," he said, and she knew then that he was going to kiss her again.

She didn't try to stop him. She wanted it. He ran his fingers through her hair first, tilting her head back before dipping his head and covering her mouth with his. An ache curled up from somewhere below her stomach, making her nipples tighten into hard little points.

It was a potent and exuberant kiss, a celebration of their safety. It was a kiss that could have gone on and on, except for Jessica's squirming presence between them.

Reluctantly Mariel leaned away from Jake. "That's one way to raise the temperature in here," she said, holding on to the front of his jacket for balance. "But I think we'd better find a more appropriate heating device."

Jake shook his head, as if to clear it, and although his lips smiled, his eyes reflected a more serious mood.

He moved away and bent to study the stove. "It's run by propane gas, and I'll need to get it fired up," he announced before taking a look at the refrigerator. "This is run on propane, too. There's no electricity, which explains the kerosene lantern and that box of candles on the table."

"With a way to cook, there may be food around," Mariel said.

While she checked the cabinets above the stove, Jake threw open a pantry door.

"A gold mine," he said. "Mariel, look at this!"

Mariel saw a cabinet filled with canned goods of every description. There were baked beans, garbanzo beans and kidney beans. There was noodle soup, cream of celery soup and bouillon. There were cans of tuna and sardines and baby clams. In short, they would survive.

"I don't see any canned milk," Jake said suddenly.

Mariel's happiness turned to dismay. "We have to have it for Jessica. Is there baby formula?"

Jake shoved the cans around. "No. Nothing." His expression was bleak.

"What are we going to do?"

"I don't know."

They stared at each other for a moment.

"Well," Jake said finally. "At least I can do something to improve our comfort level. I'm going to build a fire in here." He handed Jessica to Mariel and headed toward the kitchen fireplace, whose wood box was filled with apple logs.

Even here, far from the door, they could hear the bleating of the goat.

Mariel jounced Jessica expertly. "We'll be nice and warm soon," she promised the baby, who was holding up remarkably well, she thought.

"That goat's probably hungry," Jake said as he built the fire. "I wonder how she ended up here, or if the people who live here left her."

"I don't think anyone has lived here for a long, long time." Mariel watched as the flames leaped up to embrace the logs.

Jake rocked back on his heels. "Do you want to take a stab at fixing something to eat, or shall I?"

"Before we do anything, I'd better change Jessica's diaper. Maybe you could look around the kitchen for a cardboard box or someplace where she can sleep." She wished fervently that their cursory search had turned up a few dozen clean diapers. Jake's cut-up long johns were really not equal to their task.

Jake returned from his search carrying a drawer that he had pulled out of a cabinet in the pantry. Over one arm was draped a pile of white huck towels.

"Look," he said, tossing the towels down beside Mariel. "These will make dandy diapers. And I didn't find any boxes, but won't this do for Jessica's bed?" He placed the drawer at the far edge of the wide hearth.

Mariel was thrilled about the towels, which could be folded to the right size and were thick and absorbent.

The drawer was sturdy and scarred, but suitable. "It's better than nothing," she said.

"Let's eat something before we figure out what to do next." With Jessica settled in her drawer-bed, he and Mariel feasted—there was no other word for it—on canned tuna, smoked oysters, artichoke hearts and beets from the store in the cupboard.

"I hate beets," said Mariel, munching happily.

"Me too."

"This is a horrible dinner," she added as she claimed the last artichoke heart.

"Awful," Jake agreed.

They looked at each other and laughed. Their stomachs were full, and their spirits were rising.

"This might not be such a bad Christmas after all," Jake said, and Mariel smiled.

"There's no such thing as a bad Christmas," she said.

Chapter Seven

While Mariel fed Jessica the last bit of the canned milk they had found in the cave, Jake built another fire in the great hall. When he came back, he said, "Now that we're getting the place warmed up, let's take a look around."

Jake had lit candles in the wall sconces in the great hall, which mellowed it more than Mariel could have imagined earlier. It was furnished sparsely, as great halls should be, with a few wooden chests and a couple of settees for sitting in front of the fire.

With Jake carrying Jessica, they set out to explore the castle. A small corridor off the great hall led to the chapel, jeweled with light from the huge stained-glass windows. Pews were small, and the ceiling was high. On the other side of the chapel was a small room lined with shelves of books. Mariel looked at them more closely. She saw *Ivanhoe,* and a book of recipes, and something called *Your Infant.*

"A book about baby care!" she said triumphantly, gingerly edging it out of its dusty place beside the others.

"It looks awfully old," Jake observed as she leafed through yellowed pages, one of which proved him right by stating the publication date as 1908.

"People knew how to take care of babies then. If they hadn't, you and I wouldn't be here." Mariel hugged the book to her chest as Jake led the way through the corridors and back to the great hall, where a staircase led to an upper gallery.

They were awed by the dusty collection of armor and the display case full of swords. Rooms opened off the gallery, bedchambers furnished in the medieval manner, with immense high beds draped with heavy curtains. Without benefit of fires in the fireplaces, the chambers were cold and damp, and both Mariel and Jake were so uncomfortable with the chill that they quickly returned to the great hall.

After a few minutes of warming themselves in front of the now-roaring fire, Jake started toward another set of steps.

"Shouldn't we explore the tower?"

"Let's," Mariel agreed without hesitation. "At least we'll be able to survey the countryside from the highest point around. Maybe we'll see signs of life nearby."

The narrow tower steps were built into the wall and spiraled to the top. Jake was about to comment on their steepness to Mariel, who was bringing up the rear, but he stopped, speechless, when he stood in the doorway to the tower room.

There were toys everywhere. Dolls were heaped upon rocking horses; toy dump trucks carried loads of blocks; a sled leaned against the wall; a harmonica rested on a child's rush-seated chair.

"It looks as if we've happened upon Santa's storehouse," Jake said wryly. In his arms, Jessica, too young for toys, gawked at all the bright colors.

"I can't for the life of me figure out what's going on," Mariel said, bewildered by the array. "There's no one for miles around, and now we find *this*." She knelt and picked up a stuffed unicorn. "These are new toys, Jake. Not toys that might have been played with by children who once lived here, the children whose mother consulted the baby book, but *new toys*."

"It just goes to show you that Santa Claus lives," Jake said. He bent and scooped something out of one of the dolls' arms. "And he wants Jessica to eat properly. Will we be able to feed her with this?" He held a doll's bottle out to Mariel.

It wasn't the size of a regular baby's bottle, but it was marked for ounces and had an ordinary rubber nipple on top.

"It will work, I think," she said, but then her face fell. "If only we had something to feed her."

"We'll think of something, Mariel."

Mariel was still assessing the contents of the room for usefulness. "I'm taking more than a bottle. Jessica needs clothes, too," she said. She swiftly stripped the baby dolls of their nightgowns and held one up. "This'll fit perfectly."

"And it matches the blue of Jessica's eyes," Jake said approvingly. "Come on, let's go downstairs. I can't figure out what these toys are doing here, and I'm not sure I even want to try."

They trooped downstairs and basked in front of the fire, warming their hands and feeling satisfied with their discoveries. While they were congratulating themselves, they became aware of the piteous crying of the nanny goat in the courtyard.

"Poor goat." Mariel opened the door. "She probably needs to be fed. I wonder what we can give her."

Jake followed her to the door, holding the baby in his arms. "Our discarded tin cans," Jake said helpfully from over her shoulder, earning him a skeptical look from Mariel and a toss of the head from the goat.

"They eat hay," he offered. "Grain, maybe."

"You know this for a fact?"

"I lived on a farm once with some foster parents."

"Wasn't there hay in the gatehouse?"

"What I saw was dirty and trampled. Would you eat it?"

"No, but I'm not a goat."

As it occurred to Jake what was wrong with the goat, a light bulb went on in his head. And then he saw fireworks. Why hadn't they thought of this before?"

"She needs milking," he said in a rush. "And Jessica can drink the milk."

Mariel, looking down at the distressed goat, didn't know whether to laugh or cry. "If we can milk her, it will certainly solve a huge problem. I'm a city girl, however, and I have *no* idea how to go about milking a goat!"

"I told you I've lived on a farm," Jake said.

Mariel grinned widely. "In that case," she said, standing aside, "she's all yours."

Jake confronted the goat, who was regarding him uneasily from the other side of the doorstep.

"First, we'll have to wash her udder," he decided with false heartiness."

"With what?"

"Water. And soap. I saw soap in the kitchen," he said.

"I hate to say this, Jake, but she doesn't look as if she's going to allow you near her," Mariel said. She had stepped forward and was scratching the goat gently behind her ears, a service that was only barely tolerated. The goat, swaying to and fro on tiny, anxious feet, kept tossing baleful glances in Jake's direction.

"How about if you put Jessica to bed while this goat and I make friends?" he said, transferring the baby to Mariel.

Jessica hiccuped. "We'd better leave him to it," Mariel told the baby, who only hiccuped again. Jake thought he detected a hint of skepticism in Mariel's expression as she went back inside.

After Mariel and the baby were safely out of sight behind the closed door, he crouched in the snow and tried to get the recalcitrant nanny goat to regard him as a friend, not an enemy. He put on his most goat-friendly smile. He mimicked her bleat, softly, so that Mariel wouldn't hear. He put his hands up to his ears and flapped them, goat-fashion. But every time he got within arm's length of the goat, she shied away.

He kept saying, "Whoa, Nelly, whoa," even though he had no idea if the goat's name was Nelly or if you said "whoa" to a goat. He recollected that people talked about saying boo to a goose, but that was another matter. Did you say boo to a goat?

He tried everything he could think of. Nothing worked. By this time, he regretted telling Mariel that he'd once lived on a farm. When he'd lived on that farm, the only cattle his foster father had kept were three geriatric cows. Besides, Jake had been all of three years old.

WHILE JESSICA DROWSED in her makeshift bed and Jake tried to worm his way into the goat's good graces, Mariel read the baby-care book.

The book offered all sorts of advice, one welcome bit about how to prepare goat's milk for drinking.

"'Cool the milk quickly in the icehouse,'" Mariel read out loud, hoping her words would lull Jessica to sleep. "'Bacteria must not be allowed to multiply.' Well, we don't have an icehouse, though at the moment it seems as if the whole world is one."

"Wah," said Jessica.

"I know, I know, but you're stuck with me and Jake. We don't know much about babies, but we'll learn," Mariel said soothingly.

"Nah," said Jessica.

"You doubt it, of course. But you just wait and see. Didn't we find milk for you? And Flubbies?"

"Dah," said Jessica.

"Hmm . . . I believe that's Russian for *yes.* Anyway, Jessica, you usually make your needs known loud and clear," Mariel said, smiling fondly at the baby.

"Blfdghbf," Jessica said, which Mariel figured was untranslatable into any known language.

Mariel read more of the baby-care book, poring over words such as *colic,* and *cradle cap* as she wondered if she'd ever need to know about them.

When at last Jessica was sleeping peacefully, and after tucking her blanket securely around her, Mariel took soap and water outside to Jake.

When she stepped into the courtyard, Jake was circling the goat, which in turn was trying to circle him.

"She doesn't seem to like you," Mariel said.

"Understatement of the year." Jake slipped on a patch of ice and swung his arms wildly as he tried to keep his footing.

This frightened the goat, who spotted Mariel and trotted directly to her, becoming docile and nuzzling her hand. This only made Jake angry.

"Why does she like you and hate me? And besides, I can't milk her out here in the snow," he pointed out. "I'd have to lie on my belly in order to reach her udder."

"Udderly impossible," Mariel said seriously, for which she received an impatient look from Jake.

"Look, Nelly seems to like you, so why don't you lead her into the stable?"

"Nelly? You've named her Nelly?"

"It was all I could think of. She has to have a name, if we want to be friends with her," he explained.

"Come along, Nelly," Mariel said, holding her hand toward the goat and walking backward across the courtyard, toward the stable. The goat followed, eyeing Jake distrustfully all the while.

Once in the stable, Mariel backed the goat into a corner.

"She's practically begging you to milk her," Mariel told Jake by way of encouragement.

"If that's true, why is she trying to escape?" The goat was scrabbling at the stable wall, sending a shower of stones raining onto the earthen floor. He tried approaching, his hand held out in an attempt to mollify the terrified goat; when that didn't succeed, he clasped his hands behind his back and tried again.

"This isn't working," he said when Nelly rent the air with a terrified squeal.

"I'll hold her head," Mariel offered, grasping Nelly's neck. The goat struggled for a moment and then was still. But when Jake approached her hindquarters with the soapy cloth, she wheeled and tried to wrench away.

Mariel did the only thing she could think of. She began to sing to the goat.

"Silent night, holy night," she began, and Nelly calmed immediately.

"All is calm, all is bright," she went on, heartened by the results. Jake crept closer to the goat, cloth in hand, one eye on the goat's udder, the other on her hooves. At this distance, Nelly could kick him clear into tomorrow if she put her mind to it.

Nelly stood quietly now, Mariel scratching her head. "Sleep in heavenly peace, sleep in heavenly peace," sang Mariel.

"Again," said Jake, reaching for the udder.

Mariel began singing the second verse of the Christmas carol, and Jake sudsed and rinsed, then slowly slid the pan Mariel had brought under the goat and crawled closer for a better look.

"Shepherds something at the sight," Mariel sang.

"Quake," interjected Jake. "Shepherds *quake* at the sight." He was quaking at the sight of this udder. There weren't four teats, like a cow's, but two. That should make it easier, but he had no idea how to express the milk.

"Glorious beams from heaven above," Mariel continued. Jake thought of singing "Glorious streams from udders above," which might get a laugh from Mariel but wouldn't get the job done.

"Don't stop singing," he said, seeing that the goat was virtually mesmerized by Mariel's voice. Mariel sang another verse.

Jake stuck out a hand and curved it around one of the teats. The goat didn't move. Jake squeezed. Nothing happened, except that the goat became startled and almost planted one hind foot on the palm of his non-squeezing hand.

"Silent night?" Mariel sang anxiously. "Are you all right?" She bent to look at him, her brow furrowed in concern.

"I'm okay, don't take fright," he assured her in his chesty baritone.

"Hurry this up, she won't stand still long," Mariel sang, fitting the words to the carol's tune.

"This isn't easy, the fit is all wrong," he sang, wedging himself between the wall and the goat, and Mariel went on singing while he wrapped his fingers around one of the teats again.

This time he followed an instinct that told him he'd get better results if he squeezed from top to bottom. He clamped the top of the teat with the thumb and index finger and pulled. Again, nothing happened, but Nelly remained calm. She seemed to expect him to do this right.

By now, Mariel was starting on another verse of "Silent Night." Jake clamped his other hand around Nelly's second teat and squeezed one, then the other. Much to his amazement, a stream of milk squirted from each, hitting him squarely on the top of one boot.

Hmm . . . he thought, *I'll have to improve my aim.* The next time, he pointed the ends of the teats straight down toward the stainless-steel pan, and was rewarded by two steady streams clanging against the metal.

He was jubilant. "Did you see that?" he yelled. Nelly promptly kicked the pan, sending the bit of milk flying.

Undaunted, he tried again. Mariel switched to "Joy to the World," and after that, things progressed satisfactorily. Finally, Jake triumphantly held the pan aloft.

"Congratulations," said Mariel, and he beamed.

They fed Nelly from a bag of grain they found in the stable, and on the way back to the great hall he kept one arm companionably around Mariel's waist.

"I'd better get this milk to the kitchen," she said. "I'll want to strain it and cool it, and—"

"Not so fast." Jake carefully set the pan on one of the long tables and pulled her close. "I think I should tell you that you're one of the most versatile women I've ever met. I don't know too many women who look as beautiful when they're keeping a fire going in a cave as they do when they're singing to a goat, and I can't imagine anyone else of my acquaintance keeping her sense of humor. You're very special, Mariel," he said, gazing into those eyes that had captivated him almost from the first moment he laid eyes on her.

"Jake, I—"

He didn't wait for her to finish. Instead, he pulled her into his arms and rested his cheek against her hair, listening to the beating of his own pulse in his veins. He thought that he had never shared so much with any other woman; nor had he ever wanted a woman as much as he wanted Mariel.

She pulled away slightly to look up at him, and he lowered his head until his lips moved lingeringly against hers. Her lips were the sweetest he had ever tasted, full of what he had come to know as the essence of Mariel, and he drank from them as if from a spring that he feared would run dry. He felt his knees go slack, and he knew he would melt into her without any effort if this went on for much longer.

The baby was sleeping. They were alone in the big relic of a castle, and likely to be so for some time. The very thought of saying goodbye to her once they found their way back to the real world made him feel slightly crazy. Then the inevitable would happen; she would leave. Why would a well-educated woman from Pittsburgh want to have anything to do with a simple carpenter from rural Virginia?

He let her go. He dropped his hands, but his face remained only inches from hers, taking in every detail of her expression. For a moment, he thought she was going to fling her arms around his neck and press her body along the length of his, and then it would be all over. If she had done that, there would have been no point in fighting it. Nature would take over, nature and—might as well admit it—passion. He would take her right there on the wooden table, with the baby sleeping nearby.

But she only masked whatever she was feeling and said, "Well. I suppose we'd better see what we can do about cranking up that refrigerator." She reached for the container of goat's milk, and then she bustled away, leaving him to his regrets and his imagination.

MARIEL STEADIED HERSELF against the kitchen counter, hoping that Jake wouldn't follow her.

She had to get a grip on herself. She had no business lusting after Jake Travis. She didn't know who he was or what he was; all she knew was that he looked good in his skivvies and built a decent camp fire. And that he could milk a goat.

Which reminded her that she needed to refrigerate the milk. The refrigerator door was closed, unlike earlier, when it had hung open. She opened it, surprised that the inside light was on and that the air inside was cool. *Funny*, she thought. *When did Jake find the time to turn the refrigerator on?*

Thoughtfully she set the pan inside and closed the door again. Something strange was going on here.

"Mariel, I think we'd better talk about this," Jake said, bursting in the door.

"Did you turn the refrigerator on?" she asked.

"Refrigerator? No. Didn't you?"

"No."

Jake opened the refrigerator door and closed it again. "It's on. You must have done it."

"Didn't you say that it's run on propane gas? I wouldn't even know where to begin."

"When would I have done it, Mariel? You've known where I was every minute." Jake folded his arms across his chest and waited for a reply, which wasn't forthcoming, because she realized he was right.

They stared at each other uncomfortably. Finally Mariel threw her hands in the air and said, "I give up. Neither of us started the refrigerator. It's working. Chalk it up to something, I don't know what."

Jake checked the stove. "While you're chalking, I'm going to make coffee, because the pilot light's on here, as well."

"I'd like a cup of coffee, too," Mariel said, and Jake busied himself filling an old coffeepot while she strained the goat's milk into a glass pitcher. Soon the aroma of coffee filled the air, and she sat across the kitchen table from Jake, who handed her a mug of coffee and stared down into his own mug thoughtfully.

Jake didn't speak, and Mariel was determined that they wouldn't embark on any heavy discussions about their relationship.

"When do you think we'll be able to leave here?" she asked.

Jake lifted his eyes to her face. His expression was impassive as he lifted the mug to his lips. "I don't know."

"Tomorrow? The next day?"

"At the moment, we still have no idea where we are. I can determine direction from the sun, and I think we should probably head west, but the mountain is there. Probably the safest thing to do is to wait until someone comes to rescue us."

"How long will that be? Tomorrow is Christmas."

"No one will come looking for me. I'm pretty much a loner, and all my buddies had out-of-town plans. How about you?"

"Unless some of the neighbors happen to check on me, I won't be missed. Even if they realize I'm not home, they'll think I've gone somewhere with a friend," she said slowly.

His eyebrows shot up. "Any special friend?" he asked sharply.

"My girlfriend Ellie—" she began, then realized that what he wanted to know was if there was a man in her life. "No, not the kind of friend you mean," she finished.

"And Ellie wouldn't wonder where you are?" he probed.

"She'll be with her husband. They were going to her grandmother's in Ohio."

"It looks as if we'll have to depend on someone wandering by if we hope to be discovered."

"How long can we hold out here?"

"If the baby drinks goat's milk, she'll be all right. As for us, there's plenty of food to last a couple of weeks."

"We're lucky," she said.

They drank in silence, each apparently unwilling to say anything more, each thinking private thoughts.

Finally, without comment, Jake went to rinse his cup at the sink. He couldn't see how Mariel studied the way his muscles rippled beneath the gray turtleneck, and he couldn't know her thoughts. She was thinking that she might be safe from the elements. But she didn't feel safe from the most capricious danger of all—her own runaway emotions.

JAKE WANTED to talk to Mariel about what was happening between them. He wanted— But what was the use?

He wanted a relationship. He'd known a lot of women in his life, but he'd never been really close to any of them. Now here was a woman, a woman for whom he was beginning to care deeply, and, thrown into close proximity with her, he was beginning to see how much he'd missed in his life.

When he'd followed her into the kitchen, he hadn't planned to talk about why the refrigerator was running when no one had turned it on. He'd planned a confrontation during which he'd lay his cards on the table.

All that had happened was that they'd had a civilized conversation over coffee. Now she was sitting in front of a fire in the great hall, playing with the baby. Soon it would be time to rustle up dinner. All he could think about was how soft and willing her lips had been when he kissed her.

"Come see Jessica play pat-a-cake," Mariel said, turning to him. Her skin had a golden glow in the firelight.

"How do you know how to play with a baby?" he asked as he sat beside her.

Mariel laughed. "Everyone knows how to play pat-a-cake," she told him, guiding Jessica's little hands through the motions.

"I don't," he said before he could stop himself, and she looked over at him, surprised.

"Because you were a foster child?" she asked.

"Maybe," he said with a shrug.

"Well, here. You play with Jessica," she said, shifting the baby to his lap. She rose to stir the fire with the poker, sending tiny sparks up the flue, and he grinned at her when she resumed her seat beside him.

He looked down at the baby, who blinked at him and kicked her legs. He felt like an idiot, batting the kid's hands together and saying, "Pat-a-cake, pat-a-cake, baker's man," but Jessica cooed, and Mariel smiled. The three of them were warm and safe as dusk grew thick outside the castle windows.

"Everything's going to be all right, isn't it?" Mariel said, tilting her face toward him.

"Not unless we have a diaper handy," he said, grimacing as he felt the dampness seeping through the baby's blanket. Mariel laughed as she went into the kitchen to get a clean one.

A warmth settled around Jake's heart, and he found himself thinking that here in this castle, this strange, out-of-the-way castle, something odd and yet reassuring and wonderful was going on, something he couldn't quite explain. Everything *was* all right—maybe for the first time in his life.

Chapter Eight

"It doesn't seem like Christmas Eve," Mariel said later as they sat in front of the fire, watching over the sleeping Jessica.

"We could hang up our stockings by the chimney with care," Jake told her.

"In hopes that Saint Nicholas soon would be there? No, thank you, I'd rather keep my socks on. Cold feet, you know." Mariel smiled at him, thinking that she had cold feet in more ways than one. Here she was, sequestered with a guy who could have been a pinup, and she was reluctant to let nature take its course. Some might call it stupid; she called it prudent. She'd never believed in rushing into things.

Jake had pulled one of the dusty velvet settees close to the fire, and Mariel was curled up on it. He sat at her feet. Jessica was at the far end of the hearth, where she slept in warmth and safety. Although the castle had many rooms, they had decided to spend the night in front of the fire in order to conserve firewood. They had no idea how long it would last, and Jake wasn't willing to chop down trees that belonged to someone else.

"What do you usually do on Christmas Eve?" he asked.

"My parents and I would go to the midnight service at our church."

"What's it like?"

"Haven't you ever been to one?" she asked in surprise.

"I never lived with a family that did that," he explained. For a moment, Mariel could see Jake as a boy. He would have been vulnerable and he would have been lonely.

"We light candles and sing Christmas hymns. Afterward—in my church, anyway—people hug each other and wish each other a merry Christmas. And then we all go home to sleep, and when we wake up, it's Christmas morning," she said dreamily.

"And then what?"

"Mother and I cook a turkey. And Dad mashes the potatoes. And I bake a cake."

"What kind?"

"Dad likes coconut, and we like to humor him on Christmas, so that's what it usually is. We always have turkey and stuffing and mashed potatoes. I miss them so much at this time of year. I won't be seeing them for six more months."

"Families should be together for the holiday."

Mariel sighed. "It's the first time in my life that I haven't been with my parents for the holidays," she said.

"Even though I don't have parents, I can imagine how you must feel. Not to mention having to spend the night in a cave."

"You know something? That time we spent in the cave—it wasn't so bad."

He focused unbelieving eyes on her. "How can you say that? Your face is scratched from the brambles, we had to care for a baby without the proper equipment or supplies, and we almost starved,'' he reminded her.

Mariel thought for a moment. "Those things are true," she agreed. "But you left something out. You didn't mention how kind you were to me, or how good it felt to provide for Jessica. You didn't say anything about how it felt when you came back into the cave, after I had been thinking that you had deserted us and you had been thinking that I had left, and we were both still there."

He stared at her, unsure what he should say or do, but she took care of that for him. She reached for his hand across the space between them and squeezed his fingers.

"I need you, Jake. And you need me. Jessica needs both of us. Those truths were brought home to me in the cave."

Jake hadn't known that Mariel realized how important they all were to each other. He didn't know how to react.

"It's almost midnight," Mariel said softly. "Would you like to join me in our own special Christmas Eve candlelight service?"

"I wouldn't know what to do."

"I'll show you," she told him, and got up from where she sat.

He gazed into the flames while she went into the kitchen. He heard her rummaging around, but he didn't want to follow her. He didn't want her to see that he had tears in his eyes or to know that, on this Christmas Eve, Mariel Evans had touched him to the depths of his soul.

JESSICA SLEPT DEEPLY beside the fire, and Mariel insisted that she and Jake repair to the cold chapel for their ceremony. Jake put on his jacket and held Mariel's coat for her. Her scarf was caught in the sleeve, and he pulled it out.

"Don't you want to wear this?" he asked.

She hesitated for a moment, then wrapped it around her head. Jake stared at her, fathomless eyes fixed on her face. To break the mood, she bent to light a candle that she had affixed to a saucer with melted wax.

When she straightened, he was still staring at her as if he couldn't pull his eyes away. "You look..." he began, then stopped.

"I look what?" she asked, something stilling inside her.

"You look beautiful in the candlelight," he finished softly.

This was not the way this was supposed to go. She didn't want to encourage Jake Travis; nor did she want to give herself false hope. Tonight she wanted to celebrate the meaning of Christmas and give thanks for their safety, and that was all.

"Come with me," she said quietly. Taking Jake's hand, she led him through the small corridor to the chapel.

The altar was wide, surmounted by a stained-glass window featuring Jesus, Mary and Joseph. Candelabra holding old parchment-colored candles flanked the altar, and Mariel lit the candles one by one. They cast a warm glow over the room, highlighting the wood grain of the pews and giving enough light to read the print on the pages of the large Bible that stood on the altar.

Mariel cleared her throat. "First," she said, "we thank God for his protection, and we ask for his blessing. Would you like to—?"

Jake shook his head.

Mariel bowed her head, and Jake followed her example. "Heavenly Father, thank you for letting us find Jessica in the woods. Thank you for guiding us to the cave last night and for providing food for us and for Jessica. Thank you for helping us find this castle. We ask your blessing on all of us, and for your guidance in the days to come." She paused. "Is that all?" she whispered to Jake.

"Thank you for the goat," he reminded her.

"And thank you for the goat."

"Amen," Jake said hastily, and Mariel added her own "Amen" to his.

"Now I'll read the Christmas story." Mariel picked up the Bible and leafed through it until she came upon the age-old story, so familiar to her, but perhaps not to Jake, who stood beside her, his attitude cooperative but otherwise unreadable.

"'And she brought forth her firstborn son, and wrapped him in swaddling clothes, and laid him in a manger; because there was no room for him in the inn,'" she read. The story had more meaning than ever for her now, because of Jessica.

When she finished, she laid the Bible on the altar.

"Now we should sing a Christmas carol," Jake said, surprising her, and he started with, "Hark, the Herald Angels Sing." She chimed in with her sweet contralto, and their voices blended so that the notes reverberated from the high ceiling in joyous accord.

"Let's sing another carol," Mariel said, gazing up at Jake, and he smiled and took her hand.

"Your choice this time."

Mariel sang "Away in a Manger," because it had been her favorite when she was a child. She had become unaccountably nostalgic while reading the Gospel, remembering how her father had often read it to her, not only at Christmas but at other times during the year, because she loved to hear about the baby being born in a stable.

"One more prayer, I think," she said in a low voice, and she tried to think of the formal benediction from church, but her mind had gone blank. She looked questioningly at Jake.

"And thank you for each other," he said. "Amen."

Mariel gazed up at him, surprised and touched. "Amen," she said, and he squeezed her hand.

The chapel was no longer cold. The air was warm, warmer than it should have been from the heat of a few candles.

"What time is it?" she asked Jake.

He glanced at his watch. "It's three minutes after midnight."

"Merry Christmas," she said, unwilling to look into his face.

But he had no such compunctions. Slowly he lifted his hands to her shoulders, and slowly he turned her to face him. His gaze was hard and penetrating, the set of his jaw firm.

She shook her head, denying what she read in his eyes, but it was too late.

"Merry Christmas, Mariel," he said, as he lowered his lips to hers.

She let him kiss her, but she held back. She didn't dare let herself participate, because she knew all to well what that would mean.

His lips were warm, and his hands found their way beneath her coat and adjusted to the slender curve of her waist. She wanted to slide her arms around him, to feel the wool of his coat against the palms of her hands, to feel the play of the muscles of his back. But her hands only hung at her sides.

Her mouth parted helplessly as he explored all the warm, sweet textures of lips and teeth and tongue. He kissed her so thoroughly and with so much unexpected passion that her heart trembled beneath her ribs and her skin caught fire.

Stop, Mariel thought. I don't want to do this.

But even as the thought seared her consciousness, she knew it wasn't true. His mouth was insistently seductive, and with supreme effort, she steeled herself to push him away. For one last, sensual moment, she was lost in the scent and taste and touch of him, and then she caught herself, just in time to wrench herself from his grasp.

"No," she said shakily, "I can't." Her boots clattered on the stone floor as she ran from the chapel.

Jake waited for a moment to see if she would return. He didn't know how she'd had the strength to put a stop to the mystical flow of passion and emotion between them, and he didn't know why she would want to. This was something special, this relationship, and he wanted to encourage it, to nurture it, and to embellish it. He couldn't imagine why Mariel wouldn't feel the same way.

He sat down in one of the pews to contemplate the situation, staring up at the stained-glass window of Jesus, Mary and Joseph above the altar. Mary held the infant Jesus in her arms, and Joseph stood behind Mary, his hand placed lovingly and protectively on her shoulder.

A family group. He had a rare flash of insight, unusual for him. He didn't know where it came from. He didn't know why it chose this moment to stun him into understanding. But now he knew what the hoopla of Christmas was all about.

It wasn't only to celebrate the birth of the Christ child. It wasn't just tinny Christmas carols piped into the grocery store, or toys on Christmas morning. It was a celebration of family.

For Jesus's birth had made Mary and Joseph a family. Not just a couple, but a man, woman and child. It was simple, really, because family was the basic building block of society. Nothing could change that. It had always been that way, and always would be.

His thoughts flew to encompass Jessica. She had made them a family, too. A temporary family, maybe, but it was the family that Jake Travis had never had. Families could come in all shapes and sizes. Single parents and their children were families, grandparents who were raising their children's children were families, and sometimes people who were unrelated were families. Like Mariel and Jessica and himself.

He was overcome by this feeling of kinship. One by one he blew out the candles, and then he went to find Mariel.

WHEN SHE FLED from the chapel, Mariel checked on Jessica and found her sleeping blissfully in her drawer on the wide hearth. She didn't want to have to talk to Jake; anything she might say would only make things worse between them. So she hurried into the kitchen and began to fill the huge tin bathtub she had found hanging in one of the pantries.

The castle didn't have adequate bathroom facilities. Toilets and miniscule sinks had been installed, apparently as an afterthought, under stairwells, and every time Mariel used one, the flushing rattled the pipes into

a cacophony. She had a fear of causing a miniature
Niagara and eventually having to explain to the owner
of this castle how she had managed to flood it.

So she was relieved that there were no built-in bath-
tubs, only this tin tub. She heated water on the stove and
poured it into the tub until there was enough for a bath.

Mariel couldn't recall ever having felt so grimy before. She was caked with two days' worth of dirt, over-
laid with the smell of a camp fire and the dank odor of
the cave, which clung to her hair and skin.

She peeked out the kitchen door and saw that Jake
wasn't sitting with Jessica, which surprised her. He was
probably still sulking in the chapel, which was fine with
her. If he was like most men, his ego was wounded.
He'd probably never try to kiss her again. She only
wished that thought didn't make her feel so depressed.

JAKE, after coming out of the chapel, was surprised not
to find Mariel with Jessica. Jessica was sleeping on her
stomach, her mouth open. She looked like one of the
dolls in the tower; she really was a lovely baby.

He sat to wait for Mariel. When she didn't return after a reasonable length of time, he made his way toward the kitchen, seeing a glow behind the door as he
approached.

The door was ajar, and it didn't occur to him to
knock. This was, after all, the kitchen, and he thought
that Mariel would be preparing a bottle for Jessica. He
had no idea that she would be taking a bath, and when
he saw her, he froze, spellbound by the sight of her.

In the light from the kerosene lamp on the table,
Mariel's skin glistened like oiled silk. Her hair was dark
from the water, and slicked back, making her eyes seem
bigger. He was used to her fluffy curls, not this sleek

cap; he was accustomed to seeing her wrapped up for cold weather, not totally naked. She was so achingly beautiful that she took his breath away.

Somehow reality evaporated like mist; there was no castle, no baby, they weren't lost, and he knew exactly what he was going to do. Only the two of them existed in the world, and he was going to do what any man would do under those circumstances. He was going to make Mariel his, incontrovertibly and forever.

In his mind he was striding forward, and she was turning her head toward him, slowly, slowly, as if in a dream. Their eyes met, and he was drawn into the warm azure depths of hers as a moth, utterly doomed, seeks the hot blue center of a flame. She smiled and held out her hand, droplets of water scattering like diamonds in the flickering lamplight, and when their hands met, she rose up out of the water like a nymph, smoothly and quietly, and somehow she was in his arms.

He had magically shed his clothes, and their bodies met, melding contours, flowing together. Her breasts brushed against his chest, their nipples wet and warm, and her mouth merged with his in an exquisite mating. He slid his hands down her smooth sides and cupped her bottom, urging her close. She moaned, deep in her throat, and so did he, and he pressed himself against her, lifting her so that she could wrap her legs around him, holding him so tightly, tightly, the two of them wrapped in the enchantment of the moment....

Of course, all this only happened in his mind. What really happened was that Mariel reached for the soap, which was resting on a nearby wooden stool, saw him standing in the doorway and screamed.

"Sorry," Jake said, his dreams bursting like a soap bubble. He retreated, feeling like a fool. She must think he was no better than a Peeping Tom—which, come to think of it, might be the truth. He was so angry with himself that he brought his fist down hard on one of the tables as he was passing, whereupon Jessica woke up and began to cry.

"Okay, okay..." Jake said, rushing to pick her up. If the truth were told, he was glad of the ruckus. At least taking care of Jessica gave him something to do besides put himself down for acting like an idiot.

Mariel shot out of the kitchen, a towel wrapped around her.

"What happened to Jessica? Is she all right?" she shouted, running up the aisle between the tables. Drops of water sprayed everywhere.

"She got scared," he said, trying not to look at Mariel. She hadn't taken time to dry herself, and her flesh rose up in goose bumps. It didn't make her any less attractive to him, unfortunately.

He picked up the baby, who was making more of a fuss than was warranted.

"Time for a diaper change," he said with false cheer. He reached for the stack of towels that served as Flubbies.

Mariel's teeth were chattering. "What was that awful noise?" she said.

"I hit the table with my fist," he said calmly.

"Why?"

"I was angry," he said.

"W-with me?" she asked.

"No," he said, efficiently pinning one corner of the towel together. He was getting good at this diapering business, but Mariel never seemed to notice.

"With the baby?"

"With myself," he said shortly. "Don't you think you'd better put some clothes on?"

Her eyes shot daggers at him. Then she turned and, with the utmost dignity, stalked back into the kitchen and shut the door firmly after her.

Jake had no idea what Mariel's look meant, but he was pretty sure what it *didn't* mean.

Jessica began to cry. It was the wail that he had come to know as her "feed me" persuasion.

"All right, little one," he said tenderly, kissing the top of the infant's head. And then he added, with a kind of wonder that he was saying it at all, considering the way things were going with Mariel, "Merry Christmas, Jessica. Merry Christmas, baby!"

AFTER Mariel came out of the kitchen to dry her hair by the fire, Jake went to take his bath.

Mariel knew he hadn't meant to walk in on her when she was bathing, and she didn't know why she had reacted by screaming. He'd startled her; when she'd looked up and seen him standing there, mesmerized at the sight of her, she'd been momentarily caught off guard. She'd felt foolish afterward. It wasn't as if Jake Travis hadn't seen her body before.

She'd try to reassure him and let him know that she had no hard feelings over it. In fact, it was just the opposite. She was so strongly attracted to him that she felt caught in some kind of spell, unable to resist, though she knew she had no business thinking about him in that way. They had almost nothing in common except the baby and their goal of survival—why, they wouldn't have spared each other more than a passing glance if they had happened to stand next to each other at the bus stop in Pittsburgh.

Pittsburgh. It seemed so far away.

Mariel picked up Jessica and fed her. The baby adjusted to the doll bottle and drank the goat's milk without a peep, and Mariel was so engrossed that she didn't hear Jake when he came out of the kitchen, fresh from his bath. She looked up to see him standing before her.

"Mariel, I think I should sleep upstairs, in one of the rooms off the gallery," he said without preamble.

"It's so cold up there!" she exclaimed in dismay.

"I can build a fire."

"Jessica will wake up again in four hours. I thought we'd take turns feeding her, and if you're sleeping upstairs, you won't hear her cry."

He thought for a moment. "A good enough reason," he said grudgingly.

"We'll toss for the settee?" she said, favoring him with a brisk smile.

"That's not necessary. You can have it."

Mariel nodded toward a window. "I saw blankets in a chest over there."

Jake went to look and returned with his arms piled high with cushions, a comforter, and several woolen lap robes. "These should do," he told her. He tossed the cushions on the hearth and sat beside Jessica. When the baby was asleep, he punched the cushions he'd spread on the hearth into a semblance of a bed.

Mariel held the comforter to her cheek. "This smells of lavender," she said.

Jake ignored her. "I'm going to turn in. It's been a long day," he said. He lay down and tried to carve out hollows in the cushions with his hips and shoulders, his back to her.

"Is everything okay? Was your bath all right?" she asked.

"Yeah. I'm just tired." He threw a lap robe over himself and said nothing more.

Mariel curled up on the settee and pulled the comforter up over her shoulders. It was quiet, the only sound the crackling of the fire.

"Jake?" Mariel said, her voice too loud for the silence.

"What?"

"You know those toys in the tower?"

"I only met them today," he said gruffly, but he sounded slightly amused.

"Don't be funny. Anyway, why do you think they're there?"

He sighed audibly. "For all I know, this is Santa Claus's distribution point for northern Virginia and all points south. Mariel, how the hell would I know what they're doing there?"

"I just wondered," she said. He didn't speak. "Are you comfortable?"

"Mm-hmm" was his muffled reply.

"At least this is cozier than last night," she said.

"I'm not so sure," he answered, leaving her to ponder his meaning. Last night, she thought he meant, she had slept beside him, warmed by his body. It had felt good, *so* good....

Soon she saw his shoulders rising and falling rhythmically, and she knew he was asleep.

After a while, she slept, too, a deep, wintry sleep filled with slippery dreams. Nothing in them seemed concrete; everything was wispy images.

Until suddenly the white-bearded man from the Magic Minimart bent over her, wearing a fur-trimmed red cap and looking as solid as anyone could.

Mariel stared. He didn't fit into this dream. He was too real.

He *wasn't* real—was he?

Chapter Nine

"You made so many wishes, I wasn't sure *what* you wanted for Christmas," said the little man. "I had to guess. How did I do?"

Mariel felt disoriented and confused, and at first she was reluctant to answer. This was a *dream*. She didn't want to participate.

But she knew the man represented Santa Claus. She was in awe of him, the way she'd been when she was a little girl and her parents took her to the city's biggest department store to sit on Santa's knee. The little girl in her felt obligated to answer, even though she was half scared to speak up, just as if she were still a child.

"Well?" Santa said. "Aren't you going to talk to me? I don't have all night, you know."

"I don't like to complain," Mariel said.

He *ho-ho-ho*ed. "Seems to me you made a big fuss the Christmas when you were ten, because you didn't get a chemistry set," he replied.

She had. She was surprised that he'd remembered.

"You did okay this year, but I could have done without the sleet and the cave," she said grudgingly.

"Some things can't be helped. Anyway, don't you think Jessica's better than any of those baby dolls I used to bring you?" And then he winked and disappeared.

At that moment, Jessica started to cry and Mariel opened her eyes. Jake was sleeping, and Jessica had kicked off her blanket. It must be time for her feeding. Jake stirred as Mariel struggled out from the comforter.

"Don't get up," she said, mindful of how tired he'd been. "I'll take the first turn." Still wondering about her dream, she crossed the long hall and went into the kitchen.

The coals in the kitchen fireplace radiated warmth into the room, and Jake had left the kerosene lantern burning on the table. She found Jessica's bottle in the refrigerator, already filled. Jake must have prepared it earlier. Grateful for his foresight, Mariel warmed it quickly in a pan of water on the stove.

Jessica broke into a full-fledged wail as Mariel reentered the great hall, but Jake had already lifted her from her bed and was cuddling her in front of the fire and murmuring consoling words.

"I've got her bottle," Mariel told him. "I can feed her while you go back to sleep."

Jake looked bleary-eyed, but he took the bottle from Mariel. "I'm doing this."

"It's my turn," she protested.

"You go back to sleep," he said. "It's been a long day."

"Jake, I'm wide awake."

"That can be remedied soon enough." He smiled at her, and she sank down on the settee. She pulled the comforter up to her chin, but she didn't close her eyes.

Jake was urging the baby to take the bottle, his head bent, his voice low as he murmured encouragement.

They looked so cute together, the man and the baby, and she wished she had a picture of them. But then, she was always wishing something.

That was when she remembered the little man with the beard who had appeared in her dream. Santa Claus. Santa Claus? She forced herself to sit up straight.

"Jake..." she began, but then she knew she couldn't ask him if he'd seen Santa Claus too. She had no doubt that Jake would seriously doubt her sanity if she so much as hinted that she wasn't sure whether the man was a dream or reality.

Jake looked up at her. "I thought you were going to sleep," he said.

"I told you I'm too wide awake," she said. "I don't think I can sleep anymore."

"In that case, would you mind giving Jessica her bottle? I'll find us something to drink." Mariel moved to the warm hearth, and he carefully transferred the baby to her arms before disappearing into the kitchen.

Jessica drank eagerly, her eyes on Mariel's face.

"A bottle's better than an eyedropper, isn't it, Jessica?" Mariel whispered, and she thought that Jessica smiled momentarily.

She wondered if it was normal to bond with a baby so quickly when the baby wasn't even hers. She loved Jessica so much; before, she would not have believed that she could adore a tiny baby so completely.

"I love you, little Jessica," Mariel whispered, trying the words on for size and liking the way she felt inside when she said them. "I love you."

She was startled when Jake appeared suddenly, holding two steaming mugs.

"What's that?" she asked.

"I dug around in our host's cellar and found several bottles of burgundy, one of which was perfect for my own recipe for mulled wine. I thought we might as well try to be festive," Jake said with a smile. He set one of the mugs down beside her on the hearth and cupped the other between his hands as he sat. He leaned his elbows on his knees and looked ruminative.

"Jessica was a good baby. She drank all her milk," Mariel said after a while, holding up the empty bottle.

"Let me hold her for a while." Jake set his cup aside. "She doesn't look any sleepier than you do."

Mariel handed Jessica to him, and Jake rested her on his knees. Jessica bicycled her legs vigorously, and he laughed. Jessica cooed. He laughed again and tickled her under the chin.

Mariel treated herself to a sip of wine. It was good, warming her all the way down. Jake had spiced it with something—canned oranges from the pantry, perhaps, and cloves and cinnamon. "You two look so right together," she told Jake, and she meant it.

Jake shot her a quick sideways glance. "I was thinking the same thing about the two of you when I came out of the kitchen and saw you holding her. You look like a Madonna. Even your hair. It could be a halo."

"Oh, my hair..." Mariel said disparagingly. Her mother had often said that she didn't appreciate her naturally blond hair, which curled of its own accord, and maybe her mother was right. Mariel had always wanted straight hair, as fine and glossy as corn silk. Most of her friends thought she was out of her mind.

"What I said was meant to be a compliment," Jake said.

"I—well, I do feel comfortable with Jessica. I'll be going home to Pittsburgh after all this is over. Will you let me know how she fares?"

"Of course."

"Where she is, what her parents are like, how they live, all those things?"

"I'll even try to find out what kind of Flubbies she wears," he promised.

"I'm serious, Jake. This has been an experience I could never have imagined. I'll never forget Jessica. Or—" She had almost said "you."

There was silence for a few beats. Jake cleared his throat. "I was thinking that we could keep in touch," he said at last. "Not just about Jessica," he added in a rush, when he saw the fleeting expression of doubt that crossed her features.

"Mmm..." Mariel agreed noncommittally. She wasn't sure what he meant. Phone calls back and forth between the two of them? Letters? Visits?

She couldn't picture Jake in the city where she lived. She tried to imagine him swinging along her street, wearing blue jeans and his red-and-black lumberjack jacket, and the idea made her want to smile. Jake would feel out of place there, although she was certain that none of the other men of her wide acquaintance would outshine him. She'd be proud to show off Jake Travis to her friends. But she didn't think he'd like being put on display, like one of the artifacts at the museum where she worked.

"You might want to visit me in Tellurian," he said. "I'd show you the house I'm working on, and some others I've finished. We could even go spelunking and reminisce about old times."

"Spelunking?" the word didn't ring a bell.

"Exploring caves," he said, grinning.

"No spelunking," Mariel said firmly.

"When would you like to visit?" He was pushing her, and she didn't know how to deal with it. She couldn't imagine herself in rural Virginia any more than she could picture Jake in Pittsburgh.

"Oh, Jake, I don't know." She was wary of making a promise that she couldn't keep. She was attracted to him, but what did it mean? She needed to sort out her feelings. Right now she didn't know what she felt; all she knew was that she wouldn't mind kissing him again.

He look chastened, and she thought she might have hurt his feelings. She wished he didn't look so crest-fallen.

He sat Jessica up in his lap, rubbing her back. She burped noisily. Jake wiped her face gently and then rocked her against his chest.

He's so good with the baby, Mariel thought. *How many men do I know who would share this experience so completely?* She didn't know any men who were this comfortable around babies.

Jessica's eyelids immediately began to grow heavy. Mariel thought that Jake's heartbeat must have a calming effect on the baby, because whenever he held her that way, she became drowsy and fell asleep. Mariel had a notion that it would be a very pleasant way to fall asleep, listening to Jake Travis's heartbeat.

"What do *you* think will happen to Jessica?" she asked idly. The baby's eyes drifted shut, and Jake settled her in her bed before answering.

"After we get back to civilization, we'll have to tell the police how we found her. She was abandoned in the woods, which is clearly a case of child neglect. If they can find her parents, perhaps they'll be prosecuted. Jessica could have died in that hut," he said.

"And if the authorities don't know immediately who her parents are? What will they do then?"

"Call in a social service agency, and they'll see that she's put in a foster home, I suppose," he told her.

"I can't bear the thought of that."

"Why?"

"Because—because I'm so fond of her," Mariel said in a low voice.

"Well, so am I. I'm a product of foster homes myself, and it's not an easy way to grow up."

"I suppose not."

He looked up at her. "Remember what I said, Mariel? Maybe Jessica's the solution to your problem. Maybe she's the baby you always wanted."

Mariel gazed into space for a moment. "There's something I didn't mention," she said at last.

"Oh?" he said, sounding surprised.

She forced herself to look at him. "I was married once," she said. "I could have had a baby then, but I refused. If I'd had a baby, I wouldn't be so alone now, that's for sure." She tried not to sound too regretful. She didn't want his pity. She only wanted him to know what few people knew about her.

"Do you want to tell me about it?" he asked gently.

Mariel leaned her head back against the stone of the fireplace and gazed at the tapestries, half hidden in the gloom at the opposite end of the great hall. Jake waited while she gathered her thoughts.

"My husband was an officer in the air force, and we lived in California," she said finally, half wishing she hadn't opened this chapter in her life to Jake, but nevertheless feeling compelled to continue. She paused to take another sip of wine, covertly observing him from beneath her lashes, wanting to see how he was responding. His face showed no expression, and his eyes were thoughtful.

"My husband wanted a baby right away, but I resisted, because I thought we needed time to get to know each other."

Jake nodded. "That's understandable."

"Something else upset me, as well. He was drinking too much, and I worried about bringing a child into that situation." She let her sentence trail off, then took a deep breath and went on. "He drank more and more, and in the end he became abusive."

"He hit you?"

"Only once. I left and filed for divorce. He was killed two days after the divorce was final. He drove head-on into a tractor-trailer rig. He was drunk at the time." She bit her lip, remembering how demoralized she'd been by the whole experience. She'd thought she'd never get over the end of her marriage, and her ex-husband's death had sent her into a deep depression.

"I'm so sorry, Mariel," Jake said. He reached for her hand.

"I'm all right now," she said. "I feel as if I missed out on something that was rightfully mine, that's all. I feel cheated out of a home and children."

"I know how you feel. I've felt cheated out of a home all my life," he said.

"What happened to you—all that moving from one foster home to another—wasn't your fault. It *was* my decision not to have a baby," Mariel said earnestly.

"Ah, but, Mariel, I didn't know that all the shifting around wasn't my fault. When I was a kid, I was told I was bad for not eating all my vegetables, for leaving my shoes in front of the TV, for skipping school on the day of a test I wasn't ready to take. Naturally I felt that I must be bad, if I wasn't fit to stay in a foster home. It was easy to blame myself."

"Childhood probably isn't an easy time for anyone," Mariel said softly.

"Probably not. Though I know some people who claim to have had a happy childhood."

Mariel smiled. "I'm one of them. My parents were wonderful."

"Chances are," he said, tracing one of the veins on the back of her hand with his thumbnail, "you'll be a wonderful mother yourself. Since you've had a positive role model," he added.

"I may not get the chance," she reminded him. She bent over, and with her free hand she smoothed Jessica's nightgown. "I hope Jessica's parents will be good to her. I hope she'll be happy," she said wistfully.

The warm wine in her stomach was doing a wonderful central-heating job, and her fingertips were beginning to tingle. But maybe it wasn't the wine. Maybe it was Jake's touch that was sending warm waves of pleasure through her body. Whatever it was, it felt wonderful.

The stone of the fireplace was cool and bracing against the back of her head, and she closed her eyes. The fire crackled nearby, and the faint, sweet, woodsy odor of burning apple logs wafted over them. She still tasted the full-bodied wine on her tongue; whimsically she wondered if it was a magic potion. Whatever it was, it was potent stuff.

She felt Jake's hand brushing her hair away from her face, and she opened her eyes to find his head only inches from hers. She didn't have to read his mind to know what he wanted, because at the moment she wanted it, too. She wanted to be lost in the illusion that this could be more than a one-night stand, that this wasn't really a transient relationship. She wanted to know in her heart of hearts that a simple carpenter from rural Virginia and a sophisticated, college-educated woman from Pittsburgh could find enough in common to fall in love and make it last a lifetime.

If only she could believe! But how could she risk emotional involvement with someone she was sure she would never see again?

He cupped a hand around her face, staring deep into her eyes, and she felt the whisper of his breath on her cheek. Outside the wind blew, and the castle creaked around them. These were realities. She should have refused to be bewitched. She should have fought her way out from under Jake's spell. She should have, but she didn't.

Because in his eyes, there was magic.

Her heart turned over as he began to kiss her expertly and in a leisurely way, as if they had all the time in the world to explore their physical attraction. Maybe they did, she thought fuzzily. Maybe this, too, was a dream, maybe none of this was happening, maybe she would wake up soon.

His mouth tasted of wine and cloves and cinnamon, and his breath fluttered softly against her skin. His face smelled faintly of soap.

His hands rested lightly around her waist, but they began to move upward, exploring her ribs with excruciating slowness. A shiver sliced through her, a delicious tremor of anticipation. One of his hands slid upward and wove through her hair to cradle the back of

her head, and the other rested lightly on her back, ca-
ressing in small, repetitive circles.

She felt so confused. She loved what he was doing to
her, she loved the way she felt while he was doing it, and
yet she worried that what was happening wasn't in her
best interests. Or maybe it was. Maybe this was what she
needed—a fleeting encounter with a man she liked. For
too long she had been looking for the right man—pref-
erably a PhD—and a love that would last a lifetime.
Perhaps a handsome hunk of a carpenter and a *like* that
lasted for a few days was good enough.

Jake shifted his weight so that his chest molded to
hers, and he slid his hand lower to urge her toward him.
Her head fell back as he traced the outline of her lips
with his tongue in a foray that left her breathless.

She didn't know when she began kissing him back,
but she was no novice, taking as well as giving, until he
moaned with desire. His kisses became wilder and
deeper, and soon her kisses matched his.

For the life of her, Mariel could think of no reason
now to avoid this; she only knew that she had survived
an automobile accident, a trek through an ice storm, a
night in a cave, and an excursion through snow to this
castle. She had taken on the responsibility for a small
baby, and at times, though she would never have admitted it to Jake, she had been frightened out of her wits
by their plight.

Now she wanted to celebrate their survival by feeling
good again, by feeling alive, by unleashing the pas-
sions that had built up between her and this man, this
Jake Travis, who might not be a permanent fixture in
her life but was, by God, important to her.

She sighed deeply and he trailed a row of kisses down
her neck to the hollow of her throat. She slid her hands

down over his heavily muscled back, clutching him to her. His hands parted the neck of her sweater, and he lavished kisses in the sensitive hollow between her breasts as he undid the buttons.

His hands moved reverently beneath the soft lamb's wool to cup her breasts, still confined by the transparent lace of her bra. She was trembling as he reached around and unhooked it.

"Mariel..." was all he said, looking deep into her eyes, and she thought that she had never wanted a man so much in her entire life.

Her nipples ached for his touch, and when he rested the tips of his fingers on the sensitive underside of her breasts, she moved closer, until his hands completely encompassed the soft mounds of flesh. She slid her own hands under his clothes, and he moved away for one swift moment to divest himself of his sweater.

His chest was smooth, and bronzed by the firelight, and she slid her hands up over his nipples, gently rubbing until they rose into hard nubs beneath the palms of her hands.

"Ahh," he said, "that feels so good." He helped her to shrug out of her sweater, and her nipples were hot peaks beneath his fingertips.

They fell back against the cushions, her mouth opened beneath his and her hand went behind his neck to urge him closer, closer.

They were going to make love. It was what she had wanted to happen with every fiber of her being, though she still doubted the wisdom of getting involved with someone she'd only have to leave. And now, with the flicker of the firelight the room's sole illumination, and given the attraction that had flowed between them from the first, it seemed only natural and inevitable that they come together.

Jake's mouth was urgent and demanding, and his hands were knowing and insistent. She breathed in his warm, clean, male smell, wondering how it was that men could smell so different from women. Each had his own distinct natural fragrance, too, and Jake's was like no other man's she had known. She tried to identify it, but couldn't; she knew only that it was a woodsy, wild scent, and that it was, at the moment, compelling her to act with uncharacteristic wantonness, as if she weren't Mariel Evans, but a bolder, more seductive, more daring version of herself.

He slid both hands up to fan her hair across the cushions in a flow of spun gold. He gazed down at her, murmuring her name. She thought she had never heard anyone say it so beautifully.

Luminous flecks, so fascinating to watch, surfaced in his dark eyes. His hands cupped her face, and his eyes searched hers. "Oh, Mariel, you are all I've ever wanted in a woman," he breathed.

This is the way it should always be, she thought. She slid her hands between them, fumbling with the fastening of his jeans. He helped by lifting himself away so that she could unzip them, and he slid out of them as she shimmied free of her corduroys.

He knelt before her and slowly rolled her panties down over her hips and legs.

"You are so beautiful," he whispered, his eyes taking her in. He brushed his fingertips lightly across the soft wisp of curls where her legs met. "Lovely," he said, his hand seeking the hot center of her.

Her hands splayed over his flat belly and then moved lower, her fingers encasing his dusky hardness. He was hot, even hotter than she was, and very hard. As he strained against her hands, she felt a rush of heat in her lower abdomen, and she opened to his questing. His fingers found molten honey, and she arched beneath him, guiding the way.

She heard his sharp intake of breath as he lowered himself over her with agonizing slowness, supporting himself on his elbows as he took fierce possession of her mouth.

"Do you…want…?" he gasped close to her ear, and all she could do was cry, "Please…oh, yes…oh, yes…"

He moved a hand beneath her and paused for the space of a heartbeat, an eternity, before rearing back and, guided by her fingers, plunging into her with all his strength. She felt a white-hot throb of joy as he penetrated to her very center, and she gasped with pleasure against his mouth.

Their two bodies were one as, again and again, he rocked against her, his breath harsh against her ear. She felt dizzy, she felt hot, she felt wet and superbly energized. The thought flashed through her mind that somehow, in every past relationship she had ever known, she had missed out on what lovemaking could be, and she felt a sense of loss over those past futile fumblings. She wrapped her legs around him, lost in sensation and riding the sweet waves as they broke over the two of them, dissolving in a crest of pleasure.

She heard him cry out in exultation and heard her own answering sob, and then the sounds merged and were one and she didn't know where Jake ended and she began. As he pulsed within her, she gave herself over to the ecstasy, wanting this moment to go on forever. She had never before felt so wild and abandoned.

He fell against her, spent and sated, her fingers entangled in his damp hair. As he became conscious of time and place, he tried to roll his weight away, but she clutched him tightly around the waist.

"No," she murmured. "Not yet."

He covered her face with kisses, nuzzled her earlobe, and came to rest with his head pillowed on one breast, his finger slowly circling the other.

She couldn't believe it was happening so soon, but she was becoming aroused again. Her nipple rose between his fingertips, a small, swollen berry, and he laughed and took it between his lips, sucking, tasting, kissing. She let him, lazily giving in to the sensations.

"I never knew it could be like that," she said dreamily, and he lifted his head. His eyes were bright.

"I didn't, either."

"You were . . . wonderful."

"And so were you." He kissed the tip of her nose.

"So, if you feel like doing it again . . ." she said, because she already felt him rising against the smooth flesh of her hip.

She was ready for him, but this time it was different. It was more controlled, more knowing, and their eyes seldom left each other's. Once, when she glanced to make sure that Jessica was still sleeping soundly, he tipped a finger under her chin and turned her face back toward him.

"Don't," he said tenderly. "I want to look into the heart of your soul." He held her eyes with his as he moved slowly within her, the flames from the fire illuminating her own reflection in his eyes.

This time he waited for her to climax first, taking in the flush of her face, the widening of her eyes, the gasps that she couldn't, didn't, want to control, and then he sought his own peak. She pulled him close, inhaling the sharp, tangy scent of his skin as he cried out. He buried his damp face in her neck and murmured her name over and over again in a voice husky with passion.

Afterward, he pulled the comforter off the settee and settled it over them in a flurry of warm air, cradling her in his arms when they were both snug beneath it.

"Well," he said, "I guess this proves Santa Claus isn't the only one who's coming," and Mariel dissolved into giggles interspersed with kisses.

"We should get up and prepare the bottle for Jessica's next feeding," she whispered, but he only smiled against her cheek; she could feel the corners of his mouth turn up.

"Jessica will make sure we get up soon enough, and the bottle only takes a few minutes," he said. "For now, let's sleep."

Mariel wanted to stay awake, savoring this experience to the utmost, reliving the joy of these moments over and over. There was no doubt in her mind that this was special, that no two people had ever experienced such passion, and that nothing could ever compare to it.

But it was only two or three minutes before she slept, safe in the confines of his arms.

Chapter Ten

Jake didn't wake Mariel at dawn. Instead, he eased out from under the warm comforter, dressed quietly, and went to the stable. There, he fed and milked the nanny goat who was docile and welcoming. Then he walked into the woods, dug up a beautiful blue spruce tree, and dragged it across the wobbly drawbridge to the castle.

Jake planted the tree in a dilapidated bucket that he found in the stable. He wanted to surprise Mariel with it. It was Christmas Day, and she must have at least one gift; the tree would be the perfect present for the perfect day.

The sun was shining, melting snow and icicles. Avalanches of snow kept sliding from the sloping roofs of the castle buildings, the intermittent dull roars resounding like distant thunder. It looked as if they were in for a thaw, which meant that soon they'd have to walk out of here. The thought that this idyll would soon end, whether he liked it or not, was the only flaw in the perfection of his world on this day.

He carried the tree into the great hall, but Mariel wasn't there. Nor was Jessica sleeping in her makeshift bed. He heard Mariel singing in the kitchen, and hearing her silvery voice cheered him considerably. Christmas wasn't over yet. Not by a long shot.

"Mariel!" he called.

She bustled out of the kitchen, a towel across her shoulder, the baby in her arms. She looked radiant this morning.

"Jake, I—" She stopped when she saw the tree. He thought she would have clapped her hands if she hadn't been holding the baby. "Oh, Jake! How lovely!" she exclaimed.

"It was practically begging me to take it inside to be your Christmas tree." He grinned at her, pleased with himself. Her eyes sparkled as she walked toward him.

"Here," he said, holding out his arms. "Let me see the baby."

He took Jessica into his arms so that Mariel could inspect the tree more closely. He loved Jessica's warm baby smell, and he touched his lips to her forehead. "She smells so fresh."

"I was heating water on the stove, so I poured some of it into the smallest washtub and bathed her. She liked it," Mariel said.

Jake hummed "Rockabye Baby," mostly because he remembered that it had something about a tree in it. Then he remembered what it was, and he didn't hum the rest of it. In the song, the bough broke, and down came baby, cradle and all.

"Who would write a song like that for a baby?" he said indignantly.

"What song? Oh, that rockabye-baby one," Mariel said. "It's an old English folk tune."

She circled the tree. "What a good job you did in choosing this one," she said with satisfaction.

"Sadistic thing," Jake mumbled, holding Jessica more snugly.

"The tree, Jake?"

"No, no. The *song,*" he said. "Sounds like something one of my worst foster parents dreamed up."

"Well, sing Brahms' 'Lullaby.'"

"I don't know that one," he told her.

"I'll teach you. While we're stringing popcorn into garlands for the tree."

"I've never done that."

"It's about time you did. And we'll prop the toys from the tower beneath it and pretend they're for Jessica. Oh, Jake, it will be such fun."

He pulled her to him and buried his face in her hair, unable to embrace her with as much enthusiasm as he really would have liked, because he was holding the baby. Memories of the night before danced in his head.

"Better than visions of sugarplums," he said, his voice husky, and Mariel pulled away and looked at him quizzically.

"The toys, you mean?" she asked.

"Last night, I mean. It was beautiful, Mariel. I'll never forget it."

"Magic," she said. "It was magic."

A smile lit his features. "If that's what you want to call it, that's okay with me."

They walked arm in arm to the fire, which Jake had fed before he left. It was blazing now, the flames roaring. "I found hot cereal in the pantry," she told him. Two large bowls of cream of wheat stood steaming on the hearth, along with two mugs of coffee and two glasses of juice. "It was the best I could do," she explained.

Jake laid Jessica in her bed and picked up one of the bowls. "Let's eat," he said. "Then maybe we should go for a walk in the woods, see if we see any signs of people."

"We could gather berries and things to decorate our tree," said Mariel, her eyes shining. Then her face fell. "We can't. We can't carry decorations for our tree, and Jessica, too."

"I saw a sled in the tower room yesterday," he reminded her.

"So did I. Good, we'll pull Jessica along on that."

She looked so excited and happy that it was all he could do not to lean over and kiss her. He wasn't sure how she'd respond to such a gesture. Passion in the night was one thing, but kisses in daylight were quite another.

He finished his cereal. "That was good."

"I checked the store of canned goods. The prospects for dinner are dismal, unless you like chop suey. I wish we could eat a real Christmas dinner today," she said pensively.

"Is that one of your three wishes?" he asked her with a twinkle.

"It should be."

"Well, one of mine is that we get going on this tree-trimming mission of ours. I'd better run up to the tower room and bring down the sled."

When he left, she was bending over Jessica, the soft womanly curve of her breast outlined by her sweater. The sight of her reminded him that he wasn't so eager to be rescued after all. He'd like at least one more night with her, one more night to hold her close, one more night to—

He stopped in the door to the tower room. He couldn't believe his eyes.

"Mariel!" he called in a startled voice.

After a moment, he heard her mounting the stairs behind him, the heels of her boots rapping sharply on the stones.

"What is it?"

"Look," he said, standing aside, and behind him Mariel gasped.

Not one toy was left in the tower except the sled. And beneath the window stood a pair of tall black boots.

"Where—?" Mariel was as mystified as he was.

"I don't know," Jake said, striding into the room.

Mariel went over and picked up one of the boots. She inspected it carefully. "This boot is damp inside. Feel the lining," she told him.

He did. It was soft and fuzzy and definitely wet. Whoever had worn those boots—someone who wore a man's size 6, apparently—had been tramping around in the snow.

"No one could get in here," he said, trying the latches on the windows one by one. One swung open when he pushed at it; beyond it was the leaded roof over the chapel, denuded of snow by an avalanche earlier, while he was milking Nelly.

With the practiced eye of a master carpenter, he judged the distance. Someone could climb into this room from the chapel roof if he had a mind to—but who would? And how would he get up there, anyway? The wall on one side of the building was sheer and ended in the moat. The wall on the other side offered no handholds for climbing. There was no ladder that he could see. And, of course, with the snow gone from the roof, there were no footprints.

"Well," Mariel said with remarkable calm, "maybe the toys weren't here in the first place."

Jake turned to her incredulously. "You saw them. *I* saw them. Even Jessica saw them! They couldn't just get up and walk away!"

"Maybe—" Mariel began, but then she bit her lip. Just then Jessica began to cry, and they both hurried down the steps again.

Mariel picked up Jessica and soothed her. "We left you all alone, didn't we? And you knew it, didn't you? Sweet Jessica, how would you like to go for a walk? Outside in the snow? Wouldn't that be fun?"

Jake went outside to prepare the sled for the baby while Mariel got Jessica ready for their walk. After he'd finished, he stood in the middle of the courtyard and studied the tower above the great hall, where the toys had been. How in the world had someone managed to remove them without his and Mariel's knowing about it?

Sure, their lovemaking had made the rest of the world go away, but certainly he and Mariel would have noticed someone hauling toys down the tower stairs. It didn't make sense. It didn't make any sense at all.

MARIEL AND JESSICA, who was wrapped in blankets to the tip of her winsome pug nose, joined him in the courtyard a few minutes later.

"The snow may last only a few more days," Jake said. "From the balminess of the weather, it looks like we're in for a thaw."

"Well, it can't possibly all melt today, and I'm glad. There's nothing like a white Christmas."

Jake had rigged up Jessica's drawer-bed on the sled, hammering in a few well-placed nails to hold it. Now he fastened Jessica securely, so that she wouldn't fall out.

Nelly the goat trotted out of the stable and right up to Mariel, nuzzling her hand. Mariel scratched her ear affectionately, and the goat trailed in their footsteps as they made their way through the gatehouse passageway. But Nelly balked at the drawbridge. They left her behind and headed into the woods, Jake pulling Jessica on the sled. Mariel looked ecstatic.

"Say, isn't that holly growing over there, near that dead tree?" Jake asked after they'd walked half a mile or so.

"Oh, Jake, it will look so beautiful heaped in vases on the hearth!" exclaimed Mariel, her eyes alight with enthusiasm.

"Vases? Dream on," Jake said.

"I saw them in a kitchen cupboard. Or maybe they were big pottery jars. Does it matter? The holly will look so pretty." She ran through the snow, exclaiming over the abundance of berries while Jake, faintly bemused, followed after her, with Jessica on the sled.

Jake cut several boughs of holly with his hatchet. Careful not to prick herself with the points on the ends of the leaves, Mariel stuffed the branches into one of the many large bags they'd found in the kitchen.

Mariel rushed ahead, her hair as bright as the sunshine. "Wait for me," Jake called, because he didn't want her to get too far ahead.

"Oh, I see a fallen spruce tree!" she exclaimed, and with that she was off and running, leaving Jake behind.

"Let's take home some of these big lower branches," she said. "And a few smaller ones." She gathered them as fast as Jake could cut them.

"What are you going to do with those?"

"Drape them all about. The great hall will look so lovely when we're through decorating." She smiled up at him.

"*You* look so lovely now."

"I feel happy. As if I could fly. Watch me." She was off again.

"Look," she called from somewhere up ahead, "I'm making a Christmas angel!" When he reached her, she was lying in a snowbank at the edge of the meadow and energetically moving her arms and legs up and down. She sat up. "Why don't you make one, too? We'll write our names in the snow underneath."

"I'd rather watch you."

To his surprise, she wadded up a handful of snow and sailed it past his head. The next snowball was more accurate and hit him in the chest.

"I wouldn't do that if I were you," he warned. It was too late; she managed to land the next one squarely in his face.

"If you don't want more of the same, I suggest you make your own angel," she said, laughing up at him.

For answer, he bent down and scooped up some snow of his own, molding it quickly.

"Oh, no, you don't," Mariel said, rolling quickly to one side, annihilating the snow angel she had just finished making.

He tried to hit her with the snowball, but it exploded directly to her right, and with that she was on her feet and scooping up great clods of snow.

"We'll see who can make the biggest snowball," she said, but this time he managed to hit her, and she threw a handful of loose snow at him.

"I'll fix you," he said, and he grabbed her by the collar and washed her face with snow until she twisted away and fell in a snowbank, whereupon he lost his balance and fell on top of her.

"Who fixed whom?" she said, grinning up at him, and then they were rolling over and over in the snow. She tickled him, and he retaliated by pinning her down, his hands holding her wrists, his leg across her thighs.

Suddenly it seemed very quiet. All they could hear was the sound of their own irregular breathing.

He was aware of her beneath him, of all her gentle curves, of the bones beneath her skin, of the sublime softness of her lower lip. Her eyes were as blue as the sky, and her skin was pink from the cold. She smelled of evergreens.

"Mariel," he whispered, and then he kissed her, tasting her, tentatively at first, then more forcefully. Her arms went around him, and he felt her warmth through the layers of clothing they wore. With any encouragement, he would make love to her here in the snow, with the whole forest looking on. The heat from his body would be enough to keep them warm.

"If only it could be Christmas forever," he said against her cheek, and she turned her head and looked deep into his eyes. He was dizzy with desire for her, but she pushed him away.

"We're not acting much like angels," she said lightly.

"Do we have to?" he asked, but she was already standing up and bending over the sled to check on the baby.

"What's this?" she asked, holding the thermos he had tucked in the side of Jessica's bed.

He brushed snow off his clothes. "Hot chocolate. For our lunch."

"You brought lunch?"

"A package of saltines and some canned pudding from the pantry." He pulled the cans and crackers out of the blankets around Jessica's feet.

"Let's sit down on that rock over there and eat," Mariel said. Jake could think of things he'd rather do, but even he had to admit that they were impractical. He followed Mariel and endured the peculiar lunch. Mariel insisted on spreading her chocolate pudding on saltines. He ate his separately, watching her and realizing that she was actually enjoying the meal.

"I'll bet we can find some things around the castle to decorate the tree with," Mariel said.

"I noticed scraps of aluminum foil stuffed into a crack in one of the windows. It'll be fine for a star. And if we can find wood, I might be able to make a few ornaments. I used to be a pretty good carver," he told her.

"This part of Virginia is so beautiful." Mariel gazed at the mist-shrouded mountains in the distance. "If this hadn't happened, I would have missed sitting here with you and enjoying the peacefulness of this snowy landscape. Isn't this better than watching a football game in the company of a bunch of guys?"

"You'd better believe it" was Jake's heartfelt reply.

"What would you do tonight if we weren't here?" she asked him.

"Sleep off the effects of a huge dinner. Chop suey at Christmas may have its good points. After an hour or so, we'll have to remind our stomachs that we've eaten."

Mariel made a face and tucked her arm companionably through his. "The chop suey wouldn't be so bad if we only had some rice. And noodles. And maybe a couple of fortune cookies."

"There you go, wishing. Aren't you aware you do it?"

She laughed and shrugged. "No. You know, I dreamed I saw Santa Claus last night," she told him.

"I dreamed I heard hoofbeats on the roof," he said, completely deadpan. He was obviously teasing, but she wanted to be serious.

"No, Jake, I honestly did," she insisted.

"Okay, and what did the old guy have to say?"

Mariel could tell he was humoring her, but she wanted to share this with him; for some reason, it seemed important.

"He asked me if I didn't think that Jessica is better than any of those dolls he used to bring me," she recounted, and her face flushed.

"Ha! I hope you told him that the dolls didn't wet their diapers every fifteen minutes."

"No. He disappeared." Mariel was feeling slightly disgruntled, and she thought she had been foolish to tell Jake about the dream.

"I would too, if I were him. If he hadn't, you might have given *him* the sack of dirty diapers. Speaking of which, it should be fun to wash them by hand. I didn't see a washing machine."

"I can do it," Mariel said. She was disappointed that he hadn't taken her seriously, but at least it made it clear that they were two different types. Jake was down-to-earth, elemental; when he'd told her he didn't believe in magic, she should have believed him.

He took her hand and pulled off her glove, pretending to inspect her palm and fingers carefully. "You'd wash diapers and roughen these lily-white hands? Oh, no, you won't. We'll share."

She smiled at him, feeling better now. "I think it's good the way we divvy up the work of taking care of Jessica," she said, determined to put his previous teasing out of her mind.

"Isn't sharing the modern way to bring up a baby? Isn't that what fathers are supposed to do? I suppose that old baby book you found doesn't tell you that."

"But you're not—" She stopped. She didn't want to hurt his feelings.

"I'm not Jessica's father, you were going to say. No, Mariel, I'm not. And you're not her mother. But living together in the castle, it's almost like we are. I never told you, but after we left the chapel last night, I suddenly knew what Christmas was all about." He told her how he'd felt when he was looking at the stained-glass portrayal of Mary, Joseph and Jesus. Mariel seemed subdued, so he put his arm around her.

"And you know something?" he went on. "I like being a family, even if it's just for Christmas." He looked away across the field, his eyes on the outline of the mountains rising against the milky blue sky.

"But would you still like it if it was the same old day-to-day routine?" Mariel kept her own eyes on Jessica's face, her dear, sweet, beautiful face.

"I don't know," Jake said honestly. "And it's not something I need to think about, is it?" He stood up; looming over her, he seemed to fill the sky.

Mariel licked her lips, her mouth suddenly dry. His remark had brought her to her senses. She'd been deeply affected by Jake's revelation, and it made her more aware of her own mind-set. She had, without being really aware of it, been thinking about what it would be like for them to be Jessica's parents and to share the responsibility of her upbringing.

Jake reached down and pulled Mariel to her feet. He wasn't wearing his cap today, and his hair fell in an unruly mass over his forehead. It gave him a roguish appeal and emphasized the rough-hewn quality of his features.

"Is everything all right?" he asked, looking puzzled.

"Yes, but I think we should continue our foraging. It'll be time to feed Jessica soon." She turned abruptly and headed into the woods, pulling on the glove he'd removed from her hand and walking too fast for him to keep up with her.

She had to think, and she wanted to do it as far away from those warm brown eyes as possible. Because, now that they were out of any real danger, living together in the castle was too comfortable by far. It was easy for them to fall into playing the role of mother and father to an oh-so-adorable baby. It was easy to think that this could go on forever.

But it couldn't. She and Jake Travis were totally different types. They led lives so far apart that there was no way to merge them, ever. She'd better face up to that. She'd better not start thinking that it could be any other way, because if she did, she would only be heartbroken.

She picked up some pinecones and gathered a few fallen evergreen boughs. Jake, pulling Jessica in the sled, was narrowing the gap between them when she pointed to a mass of pale green leaves and pearly white berries high in the leafless branches of an old oak tree.

"Jake, look!" she exclaimed, glad of a distraction. "It's mistletoe!"

Jake's gaze followed her pointing finger. "It certainly is."

"Oh, I wish I had some. It would look so pretty on our Christmas tree," she said, but she knew the mistletoe was too high up to reach, and the tree didn't look suitable for climbing.

"I wonder," he said thoughtfully, "if it's the same variety we usually see hanging over people's doorways during the holiday season."

"Oh, I'm sure it is," Mariel told him. "Did you know that mistletoe was revered in olden times as a plant of peace? If enemies met beneath a bough of mistletoe in a forest, custom required them to dispense with their hostilities and observe a truce until the next day."

"Mariel," Jake said, "you don't have to tell me what mistletoe is for. It's for this." And with that he swept her into his arms and kissed her until her knees went weak.

When his lips released hers, she gazed up at him. "What—what was that for?"

"For mistletoe. And for magic."

She struggled to regain her composure. "You don't believe in magic," she reminded him.

He smoothed her hair back from her face, his hand warm against her cool cheeks. "It's getting so I believe in it more and more," he said before kissing her again.

"Jake," she said when he released her lips, deciding that it was time to lay it on the line, "this is more than I can handle. Last night was wonderful, but now I need some space. Everything's happening so fast." She looked up at him helplessly.

"You think we need a cooling-off period."

"Yes."

"Don't you know I really care about you? About what happens to you?" he asked fiercely. His arms were still locked around her, and he seemed unlikely to let her go.

"I believe you do," she said, meaning it. "It's just that I'm afraid of starting something that we both know we won't be able to finish."

"Didn't you feel something special last night? Or was it just the same old same old?"

She twisted away from him. "You know it wasn't. You know it meant something to me, too."

"Then why do we have to pretend that it didn't?"

"Because there's no future in it. Can't you see?" she cried. Tossing the bag of forest gleanings over her shoulder, she marched away from him, toward the castle.

"Who says? Why can't there be? Is it because I'm not as educated as you are?" he called after her in exasperation.

Mariel whirled in her tracks. Her voice shook when she spoke. "Let's get this straight once and for all, Jake! I'm well aware that it was *your* skills that saved us in the woods. It so happens that I respect people who work with their hands. But I won't apologize for my education! My father held down two jobs to send me to a state university, and my mother worked in a day-care center. I was lucky. But I don't look down on people who haven't been to college, okay?" She turned her back on him and headed toward the castle.

He hailed her with a shout as she approached the drawbridge. She didn't think about the bridge's construction—she was too intent on ignoring him. Suddenly, when she was about halfway across, she felt one of the boards snap beneath her feet.

She was flooded with panic as she felt the bridge lurch beneath her and heard part of the board fall into the moat. She was only a few feet from the land at the end of the drawbridge, and she lunged toward it. When she looked back she saw that a hole had appeared in the snow, and through it she spied the rotted edges of the old board. The black water of the moat swirled below.

Jake had already stepped onto the other end of the drawbridge.

"Don't—" she warned him, but it was too late. Jake's strides were long, and by the time she spoke, his boot had struck what remained of the rotted board.

Only then did he realize what was happening. He tried to catch his balance, but, as if in slow motion, he toppled over the side of the drawbridge and into the icy water below.

Chapter Eleven

Fortunately, Jake had had the presence of mind to drop the rope that pulled the sled before he went over the side of the drawbridge. Jessica was safe, and, best of all, she was unaware that anything had happened. She snoozed amid her blankets, bundled tightly against the cold.

"Jake?" Mariel called. She felt frozen in place; she didn't know whether it was safe to move toward Jessica on the treacherous drawbridge. Jessica wasn't in any immediate danger. That couldn't be said of Jake.

Mariel hung over the battlemented fence of the outer ward and peered down into the water. Widening circles told her where Jake had plunged, but he had vanished. Her heart stilled in her chest.

Thoughts chased through her mind; she imagined Jake knocked out by the fall, his body drifting to the bottom of the moat. Did he know how to swim? She imagined him so cold that he couldn't move his arms and legs.

The drop from the drawbridge was a good twelve or fifteen feet, and, despite the thaw in the air, little fragments of ice floated on top of the water, broken off from the thin shell around the edges. As Mariel was wondering how long someone could survive in such cold water, Jake's head popped up.

He saw her immediately. "The water must come out of a pipe that comes directly from the North Pole!" he gasped, treading water.

"Are you all right?" she asked anxiously. She was flooded with relief at the sight of him. And he must not be hurt, if he could joke.

"As all right as someone can be when weighed down by a heavy, waterlogged wool jacket."

Mariel knew that she had to keep from panicking. She knew that, but the sight of Jake trying to keep afloat in the icy water almost unnerved her.

"Get Jessica off the drawbridge," he said.

Mariel took her eyes from Jake long enough to spare a brief glance at the sled, which was still where he had left it. She felt torn, not knowing what to do first. It took her only a split second to come down on the side of Jake, who was in immediate peril.

"Jessica's all right," she said distractedly. She looked around for a rope or a pole—anything to help Jake with. She knew she had to find a way to rescue him from the water immediately.

"*Jessica,*" Jake said in a tone that brooked no resistance and made his meaning perfectly clear.

Maybe Jake was right. Maybe she'd better tend to the baby. Barely managing to keep her senses about her, Mariel ran to the edge of the drawbridge. How safe was it for Mariel to step on the drawbridge and pull Jessica's sled the rest of the way across? Would the other planks bear her weight?

"Stay toward...the middle of...the bridge," Jake called. Was it her imagination, or was his voice flagging?

If something happened to her, Mariel knew both Jake and Jessica would be in grave peril. Jake's rescue and the baby's well-being depended solely on her. Yet in that moment, she realized that the baby's safety was more important than either Jake's or hers.

If only she could see the condition of the broken board beneath the snow! She had no idea of the extent of the damage. But there was no time to sweep the boards clean, not with Jake waiting patiently below, so she stepped out onto the bridge.

All one hundred and five pounds of her tensed as she carefully tested each step before investing it with her full weight. Every creak seemed magnified in the crisp clear air, and she waited for the *crack* that would mean that one of the boards had broken beneath her feet.

But finally she was close enough to Jessica's sled to grasp the rope and pull Jessica to safety. When at last the sled stood within the outer ward, she said a silent prayer of thanks and ran to hoist herself up on the wall again so that she could see how Jake was doing.

But now, where Jake's head had broken the surface, there was only dark water reflecting an endless blue sky.

Her heart fell to her boots. What had happened? Had he slipped beneath the water? Was he alive?

"I'm over here!" she heard him say, and when she looked carefully she saw his head, wet and seal-like, at the edge of the moat. He was clinging to a rock that formed part of the foundation of the castle.

"Can you climb out?" she asked frantically.

"I can't get a grip on these rocks! They're too slippery!" he gasped.

She remembered the rope in Jake's backpack. "I'll get the rope," she said. "Can you hang on?"

She thought he answered, "Yes."

This was no time to wait around and clarify things, she thought to herself as she bore Jessica on her sled through the gatehouse passageway and into the castle courtyard. She didn't want to leave Jessica out here in the cold; she wanted to set her inside by the fire.

Nelly the goat greeted her outside the gatehouse and, wagging her tail, capered wildly after the sled. Inside the great hall, Mariel parked Jessica—now awake and gnawing on her fist—in her sled beside the hearth.

"I'll be back," Mariel told Jessica as she fumbled in Jake's pack for the rope. "I'll be back *soon*. I promise." Not that Jessica could understand, but she hoped the baby would know that she wasn't deserting her.

She had been gone for only a matter of minutes, but Jake looked visibly more tired when she returned, his face white, his teeth chattering like a pair of castanets.

"I'm going to tie the rope around this iron ring in the castle wall," Mariel called down to him.

"Have you been p-practicing your c-clove hitches?" Jake hollered back.

"Don't make jokes," she ordered, not knowing what a clove hitch was, but sure that she'd never practiced any.

She fumbled with the knot, taking so long that the plaintive plea rose from the moat: "Mariel...can't you...hurry?"

By way of an answer she ran to the edge of the moat and dropped the end of the rope over the side, testing it from her side of the wall with her own weight. It held to the ring.

The end of the rope dangled above Jake, and she paid it out as quickly as she could, watching as Jake made several unsuccessful attempts to grab it.

"Are you okay?" she asked anxiously. His fingers seemed stiff with cold.

"As okay as . . . a Popsicle . . ." he managed to say.

"If you can make dumb jokes, you're fine."

Finally Jake caught the rope and wrapped it around his wrist. Then, with an enormous surge of strength, he hauled himself out of the water and began to pull himself hand over hand up the rope, bracing his feet on the rocks.

When he approached the top, Mariel added her weight to the rope, pulling him up and over the wall. Jake fell to the ground and lay there gasping for a moment. Mariel found a tissue in her pocket and wiped his face. She could hardly bear to think about what might have happened to him.

He rolled over on his back, and it was all she could do not to gather him into her arms and hold him. That would, however, serve no practical purpose, so instead she helped him up. He was soaked through, and his lips were blue.

"Don't you know you're not supposed to *wear* a moat?" Mariel said as he put a wet and dripping arm around her shoulders. She didn't care if she got wet. She didn't care about anything except that Jake was safe.

"I was only trying it on for size. Th-thank you, Mariel. You did a f-fine job," he said, his teeth still chattering. They started toward the gatehouse, Jake walking stiffly at first.

"It was my fault you fell in," she said.

"No."

"I shouldn't have—"

"*No.* Don't blame yourself. Neither of us knew that those boards were rotten. If anyone should have checked it out, I should have. I'm the carpenter in this group, remember?'' The color was returning to his lips, and for that Mariel was thankful.

They heard Jessica's wails from the moment they stepped into the courtyard, and they hurried toward the great hall. The baby had kicked off all her covers, and her face was red and wrinkled from the effort of crying. Mariel picked her up and cuddled her close.

"I think I'll take a hot bath," Jake said.

"Good idea. And Jake—I'm sorry for the way I acted in the woods."

"I think we have some things to talk about."

"I think so, too."

"Later?"

She returned his smile. "Later."

While Jake took a hot bath, Mariel went outside and brought in the holly and evergreen boughs, and she shut Nelly up in the stable for fear that the goat would change her mind about the drawbridge and wander into danger.

When she returned, Jake was wrapped up in the comforter on the settee and holding Jessica. The fire was blazing in the fireplace, and their Christmas tree stood ready to be decorated. He was holding the bottle for the baby, who was sucking greedily, the fingers of one hand wrapped trustingly around his thumb.

"I'm none the worse for my winter swim," Jake said, craning his neck to look at her.

Mariel was hovering over the two of them like a mother hen. "Are you sure?"

"Positive. I even made tea and left it on the stove for you."

When she came back, Jake was singing Jessica to sleep with a Christmas carol. He stopped when Mariel entered the room.

"Go on," she said. "I like hearing you sing."

He hesitated for a moment, then went on singing the rest of the verse.

"Doesn't she look happy?" he asked.

"Jessica? Of course."

"Why shouldn't she? Two grown-ups are knocking themselves out to keep her that way." He laughed, clearly enjoying himself.

The comforter had slipped, exposing Jake's shoulder and part of his chest. Mariel stood up, suddenly unnerved. Of course he had no clothes on; there was nothing dry for him to wear. And if she sat here long enough, they would end up making love again.

It was what she wanted. No, it wasn't! If she let it, their lovemaking would become a drug, making her lose track of the rest of her life.

"I think I'll go exploring upstairs for things we can use to decorate the Christmas tree," she said unsteadily, slamming her mug down on the hearth so that tea sloshed over the rim.

Jake turned and stared after her as she fled to the unexplored gallery of rooms above them.

"I thought I'd—" Jake started to say, but she didn't wait to hear what he thought. Instead, she ran past the suits of armor, past the sword collection and into one of the large chambers off the gallery. She slammed the door behind her, cutting him off in midsentence.

AFTER MARIEL ran upstairs, Jake put the sleeping baby in her bed.

Mariel's behavior was erratic, to say the least. She blew hot, then cold, which was different from him—he blew hot all the time. He twisted, trying to get more comfortable. Ever since they had been in this castle, he became aroused embarrassingly often. Maybe he'd better find something to keep him busy. Obviously cold dunks in water wouldn't do it; after his impromptu swim in the moat, he desired Mariel as much as ever.

What could he do? Something to occupy both his hands and his mind, he thought. Carpentry would be good.

He'd make Jessica a proper bed. Or a cradle, so that she could be rocked to sleep.

He inspected the drawer where Jessica slept. With the addition of two curved pieces of wood, it would *be* a cradle. His mind grappled with the problem.

Suddenly there was nothing that he wanted more than to create, with his own hands, a cradle for this baby. He had given Mariel a Christmas tree, and now he wanted to give the baby something, too.

He started to stand up, then fell back. He'd forgotten. He wasn't wearing any clothes.

SHE WAS GOING to have to stop this, Mariel reflected as she sat on the edge of the cold bed in the middle of the cold room and stared out the mullioned window at the tops of trees.

She was sending Jake mixed signals. She was letting him get too close, making the relationship seem all warm and fuzzy, and then finding excuses to put distance between them. She ought to be more mature.

But it had already gone too far. After last night, he would only be hurt if she tried to withdraw, or he'd doubt his prowess—and there was certainly nothing wrong with *that*.

So, why not let it run its natural course? Okay, so she might be falling in love with this guy. He didn't have to know. After they got out of this place, after they no longer had anything in common, it would be over of its own accord. Why precipitate a crisis now?

At least this point of view helped her to feel more cheerful. Now she'd better look around up here and see if she could find something with which to decorate the Christmas tree. Doing that would take part of the afternoon, leaving them less time to get involved in doing other things, such as what was on her mind, and probably on his, right this minute. The memories of the previous evening were very vivid.

She opened a big wardrobe against one wall, looking for scraps of lace, or buttons, or anything else that could be used to trim the tree. In the bottom, below the clothes hanging there, she discovered several bright-colored satin and velvet sashes, red and green and blue, and she held them up to the light for inspection. They would become garlands for the Christmas tree.

After setting those carefully aside, she threw the wardrobe doors open wide, and out tumbled garments fashioned not only of silk, but of velvet, satin and lace, as well.

She picked up one of the articles of clothing and held it up to the light, fully expecting to see moth holes. Though she turned it this way and that, none were evident. In fact, the dress looked almost new.

It was a long-sleeved velvet gown of midnight blue, the bodice joined below the low-cut neckline with golden laces. Bound up with it was a floor-length sur-coat of a paler blue, also velvet.

A tissue-wrapped package fell out of the folds, and when she unwrapped it she found a small, pearl-encrusted cap and a pair of soft slippers the same shade of blue as the gown. They looked as if they'd fit if she stuffed bits of tissue paper into the toes.

Mariel held up the dress. There was no mirror, but the gown looked her size.

Suddenly she was seized with eagerness to try it on. It was cold in this gallery room, but she moved into a patch of sunlight and took off her coat anyway. In a matter of moments she had sloughed off her dirty corduroys and the lamb's wool sweater and was pulling the velvet dress over her head.

It smelled of lavender, just like the blankets from the chest downstairs. When she'd adjusted the velvet-and-pearl cap on the back of her head and slipped her arms through the sleeveless surcoat, she felt as if she were in another age, an enchanted age. She couldn't wait to show Jake.

A search through the clothing turned up a man's red tunic, which she paired with purple breeches and matching soft-soled shoes. A golden surcoat and hat completed the picture. She thought Jake might rather die than be seen in any of it—but he would have to admit, at least, that it would solve the problem of his having nothing to wear.

She burst out of the gallery room as suddenly as she had disappeared into it. She saw Jake wrapped up in the comforter, his bare feet warming on the hearth.

"Jake!" she called. "Look what I found!"

She ran lightly down the gallery stairs and tossed the clothing to him. "These were in the wardrobe upstairs," she explained, whirling for his inspection. His mouth fell open at the sight of her. Jessica, she noticed, was awake, and her expression mirrored Jake's. The baby clearly didn't know what to make of this new Mariel.

"You look wonderful," Jake said when he could speak, and Mariel laughed, the notes echoing back from the vaulted ceiling.

"Evidently the people who own this place entertain themselves with costume parties. Put those on, and we'll trim the tree," she said, dancing away when he would have clasped her hand.

"I can't wear these." Jake held up the tunic, surcoat and breeches in distaste. "This is a skirt. These look like a pair of panty hose. And this other thing looks exactly like a bathrobe. I'd look like a jackass."

"But a *warm* jackass," she reminded him.

"We can't wear things that belong to someone else."

"Didn't you say that we'd explain that we had to use their things because it was an emergency? You won't be able to wear your clothes for hours," Mariel pointed out.

"There's no underwear," he said peevishly.

"Does it matter? I'm going to go cook our chop suey Christmas dinner while you get dressed. Bye." She waved her fingers at him as she made tracks for the kitchen.

"Mariel, I can't possibly—" he was saying, but by that time Mariel couldn't hear him.

Actually, she thought the breeches would do a lot for Jake's legs. A pair of blue jeans hardly did them justice.

"YOU CAN COME OUT NOW," Jake called.

Mariel, who had been reading the directions on the chop suey label, set the can on the counter and, mindful of her long skirt, swept out of the kitchen.

"If you aren't a sight," she said, barely able to contain her laughter.

Jake glared at her and adjusted his breeches. The surcoat came only to his knees, and his tunic looked as if it might be on backward.

"Well?" he said.

"You look perfect," she said warmly. She went to him and adjusted the front of the surcoat. "The color becomes you, my lord," she said, dropping a curtsy.

"You make me feel as uncomfortable as hell," he told her.

"But, my lord, 'tis the Christmas season. We should keep it with good cheer, do you not agree?" Her eyes danced playfully, and that only seemed to goad him.

"Dammit, Mariel, it's all very well for you to play queen of the castle, but I don't feel much like a king." He tugged at the neck of the tunic.

"Nevertheless, there is this strange pagan custom of decorating a tree, and I do believe that we should get on with it. Hast thou found the bit of aluminum foil that thou saidst would do for a star? If so, please do bring it to me," Mariel said. She was enjoying this immensely.

"I'll go get it," Jake said through clenched teeth, and he stalked away, albeit silently, in his velvet slippers.

He might feel ridiculous, but if anything, Mariel thought the medieval costume accented his rugged masculinity.

Jessica grunted and waved her arms, and Mariel checked her diaper. Amazingly, it was clean and dry. Jake must have changed her.

"Now we're going to deck the halls," she told Jessica, and she had already heaped evergreen branches on the mantel and flanked the fireplace with jars of holly when Jake returned.

By this time, he looked more at ease in his costume, and he even managed to grin at her. "I hope we don't get rescued before my clothes dry,'' he said. "I couldn't bear for the guys to see me wearing this.''

"I like the way you look," she said honestly.

He picked up her hand and kissed the inside of her wrist, unnerving her completely. "And I like the way you look, as well, my lady," he said, making her heart flip over and her knees go weak.

She yanked her hand away. "So," she said, too hastily, "see what you can do with those pieces of foil while I pop corn on the stove."

"I thought we were going to do that in the fireplace," he called after her.

She replied over her shoulder, "We don't have anything to pop it in," which was true.

The whole time she was popping the corn, she was thinking about the damp flick of his tongue on the tender inner part of her wrist, and how easily it would have been to let things escalate.

But now the baby was awake. They couldn't make love with Jessica watching. It wouldn't feel right.

Mariel wondered how long it would be before Jessica fell asleep again. A baby couldn't stay awake forever.

WHEN MARIEL WENT BACK into the great hall, Jake had fashioned a big, lopsided star out of the foil and was admiring its position at the top of the tree.

"That's good, Jake." Mariel set down the pot of popcorn and produced a large needle. "Thank goodness for my travel sewing kit," she told him. She also had a long length of thread, which she'd purloined from the torn hem of one of the gowns in the wardrobe upstairs. She began to string the popcorn.

Jake sat at her feet, helping. "About what we said in the woods..." he said uneasily.

"I meant what I said," she told him. "I don't look down on you. There are different kinds of education, you know."

"*I* know. I wasn't sure *you* did," he said quietly.

"So will you quit with the remarks?"

"Yes. If you'll quit dropping popcorn kernels in my hair," he said, grinning up at her. She grinned back. The subject was closed.

The popcorn chains joined the garlands and the holly berries on the tree, along with a few simple ornaments that Jake had whittled from scraps of wood. When they stood back, the three looked so festive that Mariel clapped her hands in delight.

"When will we eat our Christmas dinner?" Jake wanted to know.

"As soon as I heat it up. Want to help?"

Jake shook his head. "I'm going to see if I can knock together a surprise for Jessica. For her Christmas present," he said.

"I'll play with her for a while, so she won't be lonely."

Jake took off for unknown parts of the castle, and soon Mariel heard hammering from somewhere beyond the kitchen.

She picked Jessica up and held her in her lap. The baby seemed to love the caress of velvet against her cheek and Mariel was totally absorbed in Jessica until she heard a knock on the door.

The noise was completely unexpected. It startled Mariel so that she almost let Jessica roll off her lap.

"Jake?" she asked, leaping to her feet with the baby in her arms. She'd heard no sounds indicating anyone's arrival, perhaps due to the hammering from the direction of the kitchen, which had now stopped. But why would Jake come around to the door of the great hall and knock on the outside when he was already in the castle? It made no sense.

Warily she stood up, and, after securing Jessica in her bed, she hurried to the door. Again came the knocking, more forceful this time.

"Who—who is it?" she asked.

"Your friend from the Magic Minimart" was the answer, and it was with surprise that Mariel recognized the voice of the little bearded man.

They were rescued! Someone knew they were here! How and why, she had no idea, but she knew they were safe. She flung the door open, ready to fall into their rescuer's arms.

But she couldn't. He was holding a sack slung over his back and had no arms available for her to fall into.

"Merry Christmas! I thought you could use this," said the little man, and Mariel turned and called to Jake.

"Jake, hurry, there's someone here!" she said excitedly. She turned her back for only a split second, but when she spun around again, the man was gone.

Chapter Twelve

"Someone found us?" asked Jake, appearing at once.

Mariel looked from him to the empty courtyard. She was speechless.

"I thought you said someone was here," Jake said in a faintly accusatory tone.

"He was. He—" she began, but then she saw the sack that the little man had dropped in front of the door.

"What's this?" Jake said, instantly alert. He bent over and opened it. "Food?" Jake said incredulously. "A turkey? A can of coconut?"

"Christmas dinner," Mariel said faintly. "He brought us the ingredients for Christmas dinner."

"Who did?" Jake demanded.

"It was the little man from the Magic Minimart. He looks like Santa Claus."

"And I look like the king of this castle, which we both know I am not. So who was this guy?"

"I can only tell you what he looks like."

"Santa Claus," Jake said, sounding baffled.

"Yes." Mariel felt slightly light-headed. She stepped outside the door, looking for footprints. They had been in and out of this door so many times that the snow was trampled into slush.

"Well, how did he get in? And where did he go? Anyone could see that the drawbridge is out of commission."

"I realize that," Mariel said helplessly. "He can't have gotten far. Let's go look for him."

"We'll need to put on our boots." Jake cast a doubtful glance at Mariel's long skirt. "Do you want to change clothes?"

"There's no time," Mariel said, rushing inside.

"What about Jessica?" Jake looked down at the baby in her drawer-bed as they pulled on their boots.

"We'll take her," Mariel decided swiftly, sliding her arms through the sleeves of her all-weather coat.

Jake bundled up Jessica in one of the warm lap robes, and the three of them set out, rushing across the courtyard. They saw no sign of anyone in the outbuildings; nor was anyone lingering in the gatehouse.

"Let's check the drawbridge," Jake said.

They hurried out of the gatehouse and into the walled outer ward. The melting snow on the drawbridge showed no evidence of anything other than their own footprints, and a gaping hole was still evident where their feet had broken through the rotten wood.

"No one would have crossed the drawbridge when it's so clearly broken," Mariel said with great certainty.

"There's no other way into the castle, other than swimming the moat, and I can promise you that no one would do that willingly on a cold day like this," Jake said, looking around.

Mariel walked a short distance along the outer ward gazing across the moat, toward the trees in the forest.

"'Not a creature was stirring, not even a mouse,'" she quoted.

"If we didn't have the food, I wouldn't believe there had been anyone here," Jake said thoughtfully.

"We might as well go back in. And yet . . ."

"And yet we don't know what happened," Jake finished.

"At least we won't have to eat chop suey for Christmas dinner."

"Who's cooking?" he asked, eyebrows lifted.

"I am. It's my turn to give you a gift, and Christmas dinner is it."

Surprising her, Jake swept the hat off his head and bowed low in imitation of a courtier. "I accept, my lady," he said. When he lifted his head, his eyes were dancing.

His eyes seemed full of light, and, held in his spell, she stood motionless as he dipped his head and kissed her. His lips were cold and fresh with the tang of winter, but his breath warmed her cheek.

Jessica stirred against her, and Mariel broke away from the kiss. Jake's hands came up to frame her face.

"You're always fighting it, Mariel," he said softly. "Why?"

How could she explain? How could she tell him that she couldn't see herself with this man for the rest of her life? How could she tell him that she was afraid that, after all this was over, they wouldn't have anything to talk about? She didn't want to hurt him.

She only shook her head, willing the silent tears gathering behind her eyelids not to fall.

"We both know it's special," he went on. "It doesn't have to end after we leave this place."

He must have seen the perplexity in her eyes, because he stepped backward and let his hands drop to his sides.

"We'd better go in," he said gently. "We both have work to do."

She couldn't argue with that statement, at least, and so she murmured reassuringly to Jessica and, careful not to look at Jake, walked with him back into the castle courtyard.

IN THE KITCHEN, Jake set the sack of food on the counter beside the stove. While Mariel warmed herself and the baby in front of the fireplace, Jake dug in the sack and pulled out a small stuffed turkey. There were potatoes and milk and butter, so they would have mashed potatoes. There was a can of cranberry relish, a bunch of raw carrots, a can of green beans, and the makings of a coconut cake.

"Oh, I almost forgot," Jake said, after the riches of the sack had been revealed. "I made something for Jessica." He disappeared briefly into one of the keeping rooms off the kitchen. When he returned, he was carrying a small cradle, crafted from a drawer similar to the one Jessica usually slept in.

"I thought she'd like to rock to sleep," he said with an abashed look as he set it in front of the fireplace.

"So that's why you were doing all that hammering," Mariel said, marveling at the cradle. Jake had fashioned wooden rockers from pieces of scrap lumber and had fastened them to the bottom of the drawer.

"If I were making a real cradle for her, it would be wider and longer, so that she'd have growing room. And I'd carve a design with her name into the headboard," he said.

"Maybe you'd better see if you can repair the draw-bridge, in case we have any more visitors," Mariel said quickly.

"Good idea. I'll clear out of here while you cook dinner."

"A pleasure, my lord," Mariel said demurely, dropping a curtsy. He only grinned at her and went to get his tools.

"So," Mariel said briskly to Jessica, "you and I have work to do."

But Jessica was already sound asleep.

LATER, Jake came in noisily, stomping his feet and rubbing his hands together against the cold.

"The drawbridge poses no threat," he told her. "Only two of the boards were rotten. Others looked as if they'd been replaced recently. I managed to do a creditable patch-up job, so we don't have to worry about falling into the moat again. Mmm...is that frosting for the coconut cake?"

"Yes. It's only canned coconut, but it's better than nothing. I suppose they didn't have a fresh coconut at the Magic Minimart," she replied.

Jake leaned on the counter. "Mariel, do you think this guy was merely a delivery person for the Magic Minimart?" he asked skeptically.

"Well, what else could he logically be? Meals on Wheels?"

"Trays on Sleighs."

Mariel shot him an exasperated look. "Whoever he was, I wish I knew how he figured out that we were here. Or that we needed food for a decent Christmas dinner. And why didn't he rescue us? Why did he leave us here?" she said in a rush.

"Because he gives gifts to good little boys and girls," Jake said. "Because we've both been good, and he's giving us the gift of each other."

Mariel stared at him, dumbfounded. "You're not joking, are you? Do *you* think it was really Santa Claus?"

"At the moment, that theory makes a lot more sense than believing he's a delivery person for a convenience store. In case you've never noticed, Magic Minimarts don't deliver," Jake said.

He eased up behind her where she stood at the stove and planted a kiss on her cheek.

She twisted around in his arms. "What was that for?" she asked.

"For hello. And this one's for how nice it is to come home to a warm kitchen and the smell of dinner cooking." He bent his head and kissed her again. It was a kiss that she felt powerless to resist.

"Now," he said, drawing the word out in that drawl that fell so pleasantly on her ears, "wasn't that nice?"

"More than nice," she whispered against the front of his tunic.

"Do you suppose it's like this for people who are married?" he asked whimsically.

"You've forgotten—I was married once," she said, her mood dashed by the reminder of a part of her life that she would have preferred to forget.

"I haven't forgotten," he said. "Was it like this?"

Mariel moved away from him and busied herself measuring out confectioners' sugar. "At first," she allowed. "Not for long, however."

"If I were married, I'd want it to be like this all the time," he said.

Mariel could think of no adequate reply. Because she was happy, too, happier than she'd ever been in her life. But it was a feeling she couldn't trust. It was a feeling that could melt away as fast as the snow, which was thawing even now.

MARIEL INSISTED on using a snowy white linen table-cloth on the table, and where she found the silver goblets, Jake never knew. He only knew that Mariel, wearing her blue velvet gown and with the glow of candlelight gilding her face, was more beautiful than he had ever seen her as she bore the turkey to the table and set it steaming before him.

Jake carved the turkey, taking his time about it and savoring his own happiness. He was almost afraid to admit to himself that he *was* so happy. It was such an unfamiliar feeling.

But now here was Mariel, and here was Jessica, and he felt himself settling into the role of the paterfamilias, and he liked it. He, Jake Travis, who had never had a real family of his own, was finding it comfortable to be the acting head of an acting family.

At the moment they sat to eat, Jessica woke up.

"I'll get her," Mariel said. "You go ahead and start eating."

"No, I'll get her," Jake said, and they both stood at the same time and headed for Jessica's cradle, near the hearth.

The baby was crying lustily, her face red and wrinkled, her fists clenched. "Is it time for her feeding?" he asked anxiously.

"She just ate two hours ago. Could she be hungry again?"

"I don't know. Do you suppose the cooking odors woke her?"

"Do babies wake up when they smell something good to eat? How can they? It's not as if they ever ate turkey, so how would they know it tastes good?" Mariel asked in a burst of logic.

"I don't know. Maybe she has colic. Do you know anything about colic?" He stared down at the baby, a perplexed expression on his face.

"I read about colic in the baby book, but it didn't say much, except that it makes babies cry," she said. She picked up Jessica and checked her diaper. "Well, she does need a diaper change."

"Here, Mariel, let me do it. You've worked so hard to cook the dinner, and it'll get cold if we don't eat it," Jake said, reaching for Jessica.

"I cooked it for you," Mariel objected. "It's supposed to be your Christmas present."

He saw in that moment that she felt about the dinner the way he had about the Christmas tree and the crude cradle he had fashioned—she had wanted to do something in the spirit of Christmas for the two people most important in her life at the moment.

"Go on," she said, shooing his hands away, and so he went. But he felt uncomfortable sitting at the big table without her, watching her changing the baby's diaper at the other end of the room.

"I'll put her in her cradle," Mariel called to him over the din. "Maybe that will soothe her. I don't know what's bothering her."

"I'm not enjoying this," he said suddenly, almost shouting, because he didn't think she'd hear him otherwise. Mariel was so startled that she wheeled around and regarded him with an expression of mild apprehension, which only made him more determined that Mariel not have her Christmas dinner ruined.

He stood up and strode the length of the hall until he stood before Mariel. "I'll take care of her. *You* eat."

Mariel hugged the baby to her chest. "I don't mind taking care of her, really I don't."

Jake spoke to her in a gentler tone. "Let's bring the cradle to our end of the hall. I can rock her with my foot while we eat," he said, and Mariel, her lower lip caught between her teeth, nodded in silent agreement. Jessica, however, was anything but silent. She was still crying so hard that he could see her tonsils.

He lifted the cradle and tucked it under his arm, smiling faintly at Mariel. "Is this what parents go through? Do babies often interrupt mealtimes?"

"Given the nature of babies, it's entirely possible," Mariel said, trailing after him with the baby, her long skirt sweeping the floor.

They put Jessica in her cradle beside the table, but she continued to scream. Mariel had eaten only a few bites of carrots when she set her fork down, looking miserable.

"I can't stand it, Jake. I can't eat when she's crying."

He had managed a few mouthfuls of turkey since he returned to the table. It was good, but he couldn't enjoy eating, either.

Jake picked up the baby from the cradle. Jessica immediately stopped crying and blinked at him. He wiggled his eyebrows at her; he crossed his eyes. Jessica appeared fascinated.

"You're not going to be able to eat if you hold her," Mariel said.

"If she's this amazed at the faces I make, wait until she watches me chew," Jake said, shifting the baby to one arm and picking up his fork.

He ate slowly, because he held the baby, but Jessica's eyes tracked every bit of food from plate to mouth.

"She likes you, Jake," Mariel said. "She likes you a lot."

"If only I were able to hold your attention the way I do hers," Jake said without thinking.

"How do you know you don't?"

"Oh, come on, Mariel." He couldn't bring himself to admit that her indifference hurt. He hoped she'd take the hint.

She got up and cut the cake, setting the first piece in front of him. "The only thing that takes my attention away from you is the baby," she said. "We *are* alone together here, after all."

"Alone—but sometimes not very together."

"What do you mean?" she asked, sounding as if she really didn't want to hear his answer.

"I mean— Oh, look, Mariel, she's gone to sleep." Jessica's eyes were closed, and she looked peaceful and contented in his arms.

"Now who isn't paying attention to whom?" Mariel said waspishly, and she got up and flounced into the kitchen.

Jake stared at the place where she had been.

"I don't think I understand women," he said to Jessica, who slept on, unaware.

He wondered if Jessica would wake up if he slid her gently into her cradle. He wondered if there was some way to warm the blankets in the cradle so that the cool shock of them after being held against a warm body wouldn't awaken her. He wondered why he was wondering all these things, when what he really wanted to do was go to Mariel and gather her into his arms.

Taking his chances, he deposited Jessica in the cradle as gently as he could. She sighed and made little sucking noises with her lips, lapsing into what appeared to be an even deeper sleep.

He picked up the cradle with Jessica in it and tiptoed to the fireplace, where a steadily burning log threw out an agreeable warmth. He turned around as Mariel came out of the kitchen, her face pale but composed.

"Come here," he said, holding his hand out toward her.

"Where's Jessica?"

"Sound asleep. I think we need to talk."

"You haven't finished your cake."

"I haven't even *started* my cake, but it doesn't matter. We have other, more important, unfinished business. I've taken your comment that we don't know each other to heart, Mariel."

She glided toward him, petite and dainty and looking very much the medieval lady. Behind her, the tapestries on the wall, stirred by a draft, rippled. The candles flickered in their sconces. Jake hoped that she would notice the yearning in his eyes, which was only about half of what he felt in his heart.

"Darling Mariel," he said, taking her hand. "Let's get to know each other better, much better."

"My lord—" she began, but he was tired of playacting. He wanted something real. He swept her into his arms and kissed her, smothering the words upon her lips.

"Is my lady pleased?" he demanded when he released her lips.

She stared into his eyes, and for a moment he wasn't sure what he read in her face. Then, with a playful look, she said, "I could be pleased more," and he laughed in relief and swept her into his arms, mounting the steps to the gallery two at a time before she caught her breath.

"Where—?"

"To my lady's chamber," he told her, and before she knew it, he was kicking open the door to the room where she had found the clothes they were wearing.

"I wanted this to be special. For you, Mariel," he said, and then he carried her into the chamber.

The room had been transformed. Jake had built a roaring fire in the fireplace, and the room was toasty warm. He had lit candles in the wall sconces, and the bed was turned down and waiting for them.

"When did you do this?" she asked as he laid her gently on the bed. The sheets were redolent of lavender, and the fragrance blended with that of the evergreens that Jake had heaped on the mantel.

"After I repaired the drawbridge. We can leave the door open and hear Jessica if she begins to fuss," he said, smoothing her hair. "Mariel, are you happy?"

"I wish—" she began, but he silenced her with a kiss.

"Don't wish anything right now, unless it's for me," he murmured, somewhere in the vicinity of her ear.

She felt a fluttering in her stomach as he bent over her, and a rush of heat rose to meet his lips as he kissed the firm rise of her breasts above the low neckline of the velvet dress.

She was acutely aware of Jake, of everything about him—of the strong, rugged planes of his face, of the yearning in his eyes. Heat radiated from his body to hers, and, lifting his head, he brought his fingertips up to trace the delicate line of her jaw from her ear to her chin.

She had never realized how much she loved to be touched before. Jake's hands, so big and capable, knew all the subtleties of touch, from the quick, deft turn of fastenings to make clothes fall away, to the light brush of fingertips upon skin primed for love.

Time slowed down, became part of her, drifted away on a tide of sensation. She didn't know what time it was or what else she should be doing. She knew only the lazy, languorous exploration of love.

Jake's skin was taut and smooth and golden in the firelight. Her lips trembled slightly, and he brushed them gently with his thumb, his touch like the graze of a butterfly's wing.

"I've never been able to talk to anyone the way I talk to you. Does that mean anything to you?" he asked.

"Where is this going, Jake? What are we doing?" She was so unsure of him, and of herself.

"We're feeling the magic," he said, his eyes solemn with truth. "The magic of Christmas."

"You don't believe," she breathed.

"That was before I met you. Before we found Jessica. Before we ended up in this castle. Before I was truly alive, Mariel," he said with the utmost sincerity.

She swallowed. He was so handsome, and so earnest, and so wrapped up in her. Was she only lost in the admitted thrill of having a man show desire for her?

But this was Jake. Jake, who had sheltered her with his body and guided her to this castle, who had taken on the responsibility for both her and Jessica, when he could have left them in the woods or the cave. Feeling his desire for her was different from feeling his commitment, but both existed.

"So sweet," he whispered, unlacing her bodice with hands that were firm and sure.

By the time he had finished, she was trembling, and as he parted the fabric to reveal her breasts, she said, "Now you," and she helped him out of his surcoat and tunic until he knelt before her bare-chested.

He slid the dress from her shoulders, then bent and took the tip of one breast between his teeth, teasing it with his tongue. He caught her other nipple between his thumb and forefinger and applied gentle pressure until it hardened into a tight round bud. She gasped and arched against him, winding her fingers in his hair.

His lips upon her breast made her undulate with pleasure, and when he felt her body start to move, he trailed a line of slow, erotic kisses upward to her lips. She moaned softly as his tongue slid into her mouth, and she opened herself to it, tantalizing him with the exquisite mating dance of her own tongue, delighting in the play of flesh against flesh until she felt him trembling with desire.

He eased her downward and slid a leg between hers, pressing the hardness of his thigh tight against her. Mariel heard her breath escaping her in sharp gasps, and she felt his hands beneath her, holding her close. She wrapped her arms around him fiercely, wanting to bond him to her, wanting to be part of him, not only now, but forever.

"I think I never knew real passion until now," she whispered against his shoulder.

"Neither did I," he said unsteadily. The pulse of his heartbeat pumped in the vein above his temple, and she impulsively lifted her head to kiss it. He slid his hands beneath her head, twisting his fingers in the silky strands. His breath stirred the tendrils around her face.

Slowly he began to kiss her, breathing little kisses along her jaw, nibbling at her earlobe, probing the sensitive spot at the corner of her mouth with the tip of his tongue. He seemed determined to kiss every inch of her, to explore all of her, and the waiting was excruciating.

His hands moved lower, over the ripe curve of her hips, spreading a warm, pulsing sensation deep into her abdomen, lingering a moment before sliding her dress down. She didn't know how he managed to dispense with the lace barrier of her panties so swiftly, but soon she shivered in his arms, conscious not of the cool air, but of the heat emanating from his body to warm her.

When he slid out of his breeches, she couldn't have looked away if her life had depended upon it. In his nakedness, Jake Travis was magnificent, and she felt as if all her senses had become magnified as he took her hand and placed it on his hardness.

"Do you like to touch me, Mariel?" he whispered, and she said, "Oh, yes," and he smiled and moved himself between her fingers as she kissed his forehead, his chin, his chest, in silent tribute.

"Now I want to touch you," he said, and he caressed the soft curls between her thighs, seeking the silken sweetness within as he drew her into a deep, impassioned kiss. He easily found the sensitive heart of her and stroked gently, so gently, until she was damp with wanting him.

"You are so responsive, Mariel, so ready for love," he said as he bent down and pressed his lips against her abdomen.

His mouth, moving lower, kindled wildfires in her veins, made her into someone she hadn't known she could be. She could not get enough of him, and she tangled her hands in his hair to pull him closer to the center of her. She felt the whisper of his breath and the warmth of his lips, and then, with the skill of an expert, his tongue found her molten core and coaxed her almost to her peak before stopping.

She moved against him, unable to help herself, and as he positioned himself above her, she wrapped her legs around his, longing to feel him inside her, but still he stroked with his fingers, watching her with half-closed eyes. It was such exquisite pleasure, such delicious sensation, but it was a kind of torture, too, and Mariel longed to be released by her tormentor.

She clung to him blindly, unable to speak, unable to move, totally in his thrall, until with a victorious cry he filled all the emptiness she had ever known with his own hard and satisfying need. She heard him cry out, speak her name, but she wasn't really conscious; all she wanted was to feel and feel and feel, to be entered again and again in time to the elemental rhythm pounding in her veins, to give herself so completely to this man that she would never again be the same person she was now, not ever.

He was much more aware than she, much more ready to pace himself to her passion. They found a flow, a way of giving and receiving happiness, that surpassed the ordinary and approached the sublime.

At the moment when Jake pushed a damp strand of hair away from Mariel's face, their eyes met, completing their union. His eyes were so dark that Mariel could see no iris; all she saw was the reflection of her face, blurred with passion, in their depths. At that moment, with a fusion of spirit, a meshing of bodies, a blending of souls, their climax exploded inward and outward, leaving them drowning and helpless, safe in each other's arms.

Mariel was limp with exhaustion, but at the same time she felt a fierce, proud joy in her heart at what she and Jake had achieved together. They had transcended the boundaries that usually separate two people and had become one in a state of mind and body that she knew was the rarest of human accomplishments. She nestled close to him, as if by maintaining a connection she could make this moment last forever.

She must have slept, though she didn't know how long. When she awoke, Jake's arms still held her close. She thought she would like to lie just this way in his arms forever, languidly savoring the joy of their mating. She was just beginning, slowly and lazily to figure out the implications of this feeling when she heard the explosion outside the chamber window.

She was alert instantly. Jake jumped to his feet.

"What was that?" she asked, clutching the covers to her breasts.

"Gunfire, I think. Someone is shooting outside the castle!"

Chapter Thirteen

Mariel struggled into her sweater and slacks, and Jake raced downstairs to Jessica, who had been awakened by the gunshots. The baby was screaming at the top of her lungs.

Mariel had barely reached them when there was a loud pounding on the door. Mariel looked wildly at Jake, who was zipping up his jeans, grim-faced.

"Who do you think it is?" she said.

"It doesn't sound like some kindly, mild-mannered old gentleman with a beard," Jake replied, his voice muffled by the turtleneck he was pulling over his head.

"Are you going to the door?" Outside, someone was shouting, and they heard another blast of gunfire.

"I'd better, or they'll break it down."

Mariel picked up the crying Jessica and cradled her in her arms. "Hush. Everything's all right," Mariel said, though she did not quite believe it herself.

Jake was at the door now. "Who is it?"

"Open up, open up, we want to wish you a merry Christmas!" was the shouted demand.

Suddenly Jake's features lit with recognition and relief. "It's okay," he said to Mariel. "They mean us no harm."

"But they're shooting guns! What are they doing here?" Mariel said, shocked that Jake was going to open the door without asking more questions.

Jake shot the bolt. "Quaint local custom," he said, smiling broadly. "You'll see." To Mariel's dismay, he flung the door wide.

It was dark, and a full moon illuminated the scene. Mariel could make out one or two grinning male faces, and other people, men and boys, carrying old-fashioned muskets, were milling in the courtyard, laughing and jostling one another.

"Merry Christmas! Merry Christmas!" they shouted when they saw Jake, Mariel and the baby in the doorway.

"Where is Mr. Nicholas? Is he home?" asked one of the party.

"Won't you come in?" said Jake, and Mariel stared at him in disbelief.

"Jake—" she said, but he quieted her with a glance.

"Ah, it's a cold night. We don't mind if we do," said the leader, and Mariel had no choice but to stand back as twelve men and boys trooped past and headed for the fireplace.

The leader looked from Jake to Mariel and held out his hand. "I'm Barney Sims," he said.

"Jake Travis. This is Mariel, and the baby is Jessica. Frankly, we need your help."

"What can we do for you?"

"Mariel, please, will you make us some hot chocolate?" Jake asked. So Mariel listened from the kitchen, Jessica propped against her shoulder, while she stirred hot chocolate and Jake told Barney Sims and his party the story of their accident, being lost in the woods, and their subsequent walk to the deserted castle.

When she came out of the kitchen, she arranged the now-sleepy Jessica in her cradle and carried in a tray holding cups of hot chocolate.

"Funny, I thought it was, when we saw a light on the second floor of the gatehouse. We didn't expect anyone to be here," said Barney.

"A light in the second story of the gatehouse? We didn't—couldn't have—put a light in the gatehouse. The stairs aren't—" Mariel began, but Jake threw her a warning look. It said, *Don't tell crazy stories.* It said, *Don't tell them something they won't—or can't—believe.*

"Mr. Nicholas, the old guy who owns this place, usually goes away during the winter, but somehow I had a hunch I'd better check on him. He's an old fellow, you know, and healthy enough, but neighbor looks after neighbor around here," said Barney, oblivious of the byplay between Mariel and Jake.

"Neighbors? We didn't see any houses around," Mariel said.

"We came by Jeep. It's not easy to get in and out of this place," he said. That was certainly not news.

"If only we could have found you when we were lost," Mariel said, sitting down on the hearth beside Jake.

"We live on the other side of the mountain," said Barney Sims.

"Can you give us a ride into Tellurian tonight?" Jake asked.

"Wish we could," one of the men said, "but we've got three Jeeploads with just the bunch of us, and bags of mistletoe to take back besides, and no room left over for three more people. What we'd better do is send a

Jeep in tomorrow morning. You're safe here for the night, aren't you?"

"Safe enough," Jake said.

Jake went to make more hot chocolate. Mariel leaned forward, eager to talk to the men about their reason for roaming around on Christmas night, shooting off old muskets.

"It's tradition, that's all I know," Barney Sims said, clearly warming toward her. "I heard it started when the old-timers went to gather mistletoe. It grows so high no one could climb up and get it, so they had to shoot it down."

"But why on Christmas Day? Why not before?" Mariel asked.

"The mistletoe's got to be fresh for the big party on Christmas night," said one of the boys.

"Yeah, the women like to hang it up so they get plenty of kissing."

"Aw, Barney, it's not just the women who like the kissing," said one of the men.

As a collector of Christmas folklore, Mariel didn't often find something totally new, and yet she had never heard of this custom before. She borrowed a piece of paper and a pen from one of the men and wrote down everything they could tell her about the origin of the custom of shooting down the mistletoe, scribbling until they said they had to go.

"Look for the Jeep early in the morning," Barney said by way of parting. "We'll get you and your family out of here, safe and sound."

Mariel hung back, busying herself with Jessica, until the visitors had gone and Jake had returned.

"Well," he said with a certain finality. "We're rescued, Mariel."

"Yes," she said in a curiously flat tone, her excitement having evaporated now that reality was beginning to sink in. "I suppose we are."

He waited until she laid Jessica in her cradle before pulling her down beside him on the hearth.

"In a way," he said, gently taking her hand in his, "I've felt rescued ever since I met you."

She tried to pull her hand away. She wasn't up to any declarations right now. Her lips were still swollen from his passionate kisses, and her body was still primed for love.

"Mariel, listen to me," he said. She would have turned away, but he grasped her by the shoulders and made her look at him.

"Mariel," he said. "I never thought I'd be in love with anyone, but what has happened between us has changed my mind. I'm crazy about you, Mariel. When we came out of that cave into a world all fresh and new, it was as if I'd left the dark part of my life behind, too. I don't want to let you go. If we were together, every day could be like Christmas."

"I don't know what to say," she said, helpless under the restless scrutiny of those warm brown eyes.

"Say you feel the same way," he urged. "Say you love me."

"I—I *want* to say it," she told him, and he relaxed his grip on her shoulders and pulled her into his arms. She heard his heartbeat—or was it hers? She couldn't distinguish whose was whose anymore.

"Then why don't you make us both very happy? It's only three little words. Three very simple, easy words. You love me, Mariel. You know you do!" He held her fiercely, and she couldn't see his face.

"If I say it, then we have to do something about it. You have your life, and I have mine."

"We can combine them. I know we can! You and me and the baby—"

"She isn't our baby, Jake," Mariel said quietly. "Have you forgotten that?"

He eased away so that he could look at Jessica and then back to Mariel. "I *have* forgotten, yes, in the same way I've forgotten what my life was like before I had you."

"You were the one who kept reminding me at first that Jessica has parents somewhere," Mariel said, perilously near tears.

"We could have lots of babies of our own."

"It's what I've always wanted, a home and children," Mariel said. "But how can I make any promises? Everything has seemed so unreal, with toys disappearing and roly-poly little men showing up and then leaving without a trace, and men shooting muskets in the courtyard. How can I know if what we feel is real, Jake? How can I?" Tears began to run down her face, and he gathered her in his arms.

"It's real, believe me," he said. "As real as what we feel when I do this."

He kissed her. It was a long, sweet, lingering kiss that spoke of caring and passion and happiness to come. It promised forever and eternity and a life filled with love. And magic. It captured all the magic of the hours they had spent together and made it seem, in that moment, more real than anything else in Mariel's life.

But the kiss ended. As their life together would end tomorrow.

In a moment, she was sobbing in his arms, and he was kissing and consoling her, and all she could think of was that here was an eligible, handsome, kind, considerate man, and she was a fool for not telling him she loved him. But she couldn't lie. She didn't know if she loved him or not.

He lifted her in his arms. "Come to bed," he said, and she made no objection.

He carried her upstairs, this time setting her down gently amid the rumpled, sweet-scented sheets, adding another log to the fire before covering her body with his. Sparks flew up the chimney like golden fireflies, and Mariel held him in her arms and watched them go, like so many memories turning to ash.

After a while, he kissed her face tenderly. Her tears were wet against his lips. Then, because they couldn't help it, because this was to be their last night in the castle, they coupled, slowly and gently, in a celebration of their time together.

To Mariel, who was lost in a haze of desire, the scene had a dreamlike quality of illusion—Jake's dear, wonderful face hovering above her, the candlelight and fireglow playing across the curves and planes of their bodies, shadows leaping and blending on the wall. There was delicious excitement and overwhelming passion; there was joy and exuberance, and finally peace.

That night they slept in each other's arms, waking and sleeping, making love and just looking at each other, whispering and murmuring all the age-old endearments that lovers have shared in their mutual enchantment since the beginning of time. In the castle they were secluded, lost, far away from mundane worries. Tonight, they didn't have to think about tomorrow and the changes it would bring. Tonight, all they had to do was love.

When the pearly light of dawn crept into the room, Mariel was startled awake.

Jessica, she thought, alarmed. Jessica hadn't cried all night.

Jake was lying with his head pillowed on her shoulder, one hand thrown carelessly across her breast. Carefully she lifted his hand and set it aside, and he whispered her name. Her hair spread across his chest like a golden cloak, and he stirred when she slid out from under the robe covering them.

But he didn't wake up, and, mindful of her responsibility to the baby, Mariel clutched another blanket around her shoulders and crept down the stairs to the great hall.

Jessica was sleeping peacefully, and Mariel realized that the infant had slept through the night. This was a milestone her friends had often mentioned when talking about their own babies.

Mariel went swiftly into the kitchen and warmed Jessica's bottle, wondering as she heated the milk what would happen to the goat when they left. They would have to send someone to get Nelly; otherwise, she might starve. Unless the owner of this place returned, and Mariel didn't know how likely that was.

Mr. Nicholas, the mistletoe shooters had called him. They hadn't seemed to know him well, though they had appeared to like him well enough. Mr. *Who* Nicholas? Mariel wondered. They hadn't given him a first name.

Jessica woke up while Mariel was warming the bottle. As she gathered the baby into her arms, Mariel was glad that she was awake before Jake so that she and Jessica could enjoy this moment of closeness together.

"Jessica," Mariel said, and Jessica seemed to recognize her name. A sense of melancholy settled over

Mariel. What was Jessica's real name? Or what name would foster parents give her, assuming that her real parents couldn't be found?

Mariel knew she'd always remember Jessica, how her warm little body snuggled so close, how her tiny, seeking mouth had pushed against her breasts on that first night in the cave. Now that she had sampled motherhood, it was going to be hard to give it up.

She held Jessica over her shoulder and burped her, then settled her in her lap again. Jessica was dressed in doll clothes from the tower room. She looked so pretty, the pink of her cheeks echoed in the pink of the polkadot flannel doll's nightgown she wore.

When Jessica had drained the bottle, Mariel couldn't bear to put her back into her cradle. Instead, she carried her upstairs to the room she had shared with Jake.

Jake had been up to put another log on the fire, and he was sitting up in bed when Mariel came in.

"Good morning," he said, smiling at them. The sun had risen so that a slat of lemony light lay across the pillow, which he patted invitingly. Mariel climbed up on the bed and laid Jessica between them.

"What time to you think the Jeep will come?" Mariel asked.

"I don't know. Barney Sims said it would be early," Jake replied.

"We should get dressed," said Mariel.

"We should," he agreed, sliding his arm around her and pulling her close.

"Jake..."

"I just want to feel your skin next to mine."

"It leads to other things."

"Only this, at the moment," he said capturing her lips for a kiss.

She pulled away. "We'd better eat breakfast."

"I'm not hungry." He slid a hand around her neck and pulled her down beside him on the pillow. "You mean so much to me. I really do want to keep seeing you," he said, gazing deep into her eyes, as if he were trying to work his way into her very soul.

"We will," she said helplessly, though she knew it wasn't true.

"Wouldn't you like to see each other? Say in a couple of weeks, in order to catch up?"

"I—I'm not sure," she hedged.

Jake was silent for several minutes. "I'm not going to pressure you," he said finally. "But I know—and I hope you know—that I'm not going to change my mind. I'm not going to stop loving you." *And I'm not going to let you get away with this,* he thought. If Mariel noticed the determined set of his chin, she gave no sign.

Between them, Jessica stirred. Mariel sat up and took the baby into her arms.

Jake felt a wave of longing wash over him. "That's the way I want to remember you," he said softly. "With the baby in your arms, looking like a Madonna."

"Please, will you hold her while I get dressed?" Mariel asked. She was on the verge of tears.

Jake nodded, his eyes bright, his look solemn, and she shifted the baby into his arms. Clutching the blanket around her, she slid out of bed.

He watched her as she dressed, and once he said, "You're the most beautiful woman I've ever seen, Mariel," but all she could do was look at him. She didn't want to provide any encouragement for him to think that they had a future together, because she didn't think they did.

Later, she cooked a makeshift breakfast while Jessica watched from her cradle. Jake replanted the Christmas tree in the woods and, using pen and paper borrowed from their visitors, wrote a note to the owner of the castle, scrawling his name and address at the bottom so that he could be charged for the items they had used. He left the note under a salt shaker in the kitchen. Mariel was washing up their coffee cups when they heard the honk of a horn at the drawbridge. At the sound, she felt a sense of impending doom. She had known it was coming, but she couldn't welcome it.

"Whoever is driving the Jeep probably doesn't want to attempt the drawbridge," said Jake grimly, and he went to talk to the person, who came back with him a few minutes later.

"Mariel, this is Barney's cousin, Hoke Sims," he said, his voice neutral, not giving away his feelings. "He's going to take us to Tellurian."

Mariel said hello, and Jake shrugged into his backpack. He held Mariel's coat for her, and they looked around the great hall one last time. They avoided looking at each other.

"Big old barn of a place, this castle," said Hoke Sims. "Big old *ugly* place, if you ask me."

"Oh, you get used to it," Mariel said.

Jake gave her a sharp look. "I'll carry Jessica out," he said, going to get the baby.

"I want to take a last look around. To see if I left anything."

Jake spared her a curt nod, and he and Hoke Sims went out, leaving her alone in the great hall.

Mariel fought to gain control of herself. She wasn't going to cry; she wasn't going to let her emotions run away with her. She blinked back tears, and when her vision cleared, she found herself staring at the tapestries hanging on the wall.

To her regret, Mariel had never taken the time to look closely at the tapestries before. Now, while she was trying to quell her tears, while she listened to Jake and Hoke outside the door, discussing what to do about Nelly the goat, she couldn't help but notice them.

At this early hour, a shaft of light from one of the narrow windows illuminated the wall hangings, making the rich embroidery gleam. At first, the illustrations on the fabric seemed to be standard tapestry fare—a unicorn surrounded by a group of ladies, a formation of knights and a depiction of a joust, a dancing bear and a juggler in a great hall that resembled this one.

"Mariel? It's time to go," Jake said from the door, propping it open. Jessica was in his arms, wrapped warmly in her pink wool blanket.

"One moment," she called back, wiping her eyes, her back turned to him. "I've been wanting to take a look at these ever since I got here."

She had reached the last tapestry and was ready to turn around when she noticed that it was different from the others. No veiled ladies here, and no knights, just an artistic view of a castle that looked very much like this one. A drawbridge, a moat, a strikingly similar gatehouse and—

"Jake!" she called uncertainly. "Come look at this!"

But the door swung on a cold wind that swept through the hall. Jake had left, presumably to go to the Jeep. She heard the Jeep's motor start up, and she knew that it was no use to call Jake.

She took one last look at the tapestry, which pictured something she knew she would never forget.

"Mariel," called Jake.

She had to leave. Her time here was over. One last look around the great hall, and then she pulled the door firmly shut behind her.

"What took you so long?" Jake asked from the back seat as she climbed into the front seat of the Jeep.

"Just looking around one last time," she said.

"And what did you see?"

"The tapestries. By the way, what did you decide to do about Nelly?" she asked briefly, leaning over and chucking Jessica under the chin. The baby looked so sweet, her cheeks pink and glowing, her eyes wide and wondering.

"I suspect that she belongs to my brother-in-law," said Hoke. "He has a herd of goats, and this one probably wandered away."

"In winter? During two violent storms?" murmured Mariel, who found this hypothesis unlikely.

"We thought that the goat might belong to the castle's owner," Jake said.

"To Mr. Nicholas? No, he's not here enough to keep any animals, though he used to breed some kind of exotic deer," Hoke said. The Jeep bumped over a rutted track, now turned to mud with the thaw.

"Tell me about this Mr. Nicholas," Mariel said.

"Oh, he's a nice guy, but a recluse of sorts. No one sees him much."

"He's away most of the winter?" Mariel ventured.

"Yeah, that's what I've always heard. The rumor is that his family won a lottery in Europe years ago, and the present Mr. Nicholas's father was a student of medieval studies. He built the castle on a kind of a whim, and he lived here for a long time. In fact, I think he was the one who started breeding the deer."

"What kind of deer?" Jake asked.

"Reindeer," Mariel said under her breath, and Jake looked at her sharply.

Hoke, who seemed not to have heard, shook his head. "No one knows. You hardly ever saw them. Maybe a glimpse now and then through the trees, that's all, according to my grandfather, who knew Mr. Nicholas's dad. The deer didn't like to be around people much."

"When do you expect this Mr. Nicholas back?" Jake asked.

"Who knows? He's a hard guy to figure. Kind of eccentric, and all that," Hoke said philosophically.

They rode on another mile or two, and Mariel mulled it all over. There were no firm answers, but she thought she knew who the mysterious owner of the castle was. She didn't think she could talk to this Hoke Sims about it. No, she'd better keep quiet.

"I'd like to hold Jessica," she said after a while, and Jake handed the baby over the seat. Mariel buried her face in the infant's neck, telling herself that her eyes were watering from the cold. Behind her, Jake rode silently, his eyes on the back of her head. They didn't speak to each other all the way into town.

"So," JAKE SAID in front of the Department of Social Services office building as Mariel was about to get in the car she had rented, "you won't change your mind and come see my house?" His southern drawl seemed even more Southern than usual; she had grown so accustomed to it that she'd almost forgotten about it.

"I want to go home," she said, keeping her eyes on the distant mountains.

"The social worker was good with Jessica, don't you think?" Jake asked. They'd had to answer a battery of suspicious questions, but finally, because of their sincerity, they'd been believed. *Yes,* Jake and Mariel had said when interviewed separately and together, *we really found this baby in the woods. No,* they had both said, *we don't know who she is or where her parents are.* Because there was no evidence to the contrary, and because Jessica had obviously been well cared for, the social worker had taken their word about what had happened and found a foster home for Jessica immediately.

"I hope the foster family will take good care of her," Mariel said. She had seen the foster mother and father when they had come to pick up Jessica at the Department of Social Services. They had both had kind faces.

"I'll check up on it," Jake said. "I'll be in touch with you."

Mariel managed a weak smile. "Do you suppose they'll find someone to adopt her right away?"

"They'll have to wait until they're sure they can't locate her parents," Jake reminded her.

"If you hear that they're going to let her be adopted, will you let me know?"

"Of course. Any chance you'd want her?"

"If they'd let a single mother adopt her, I'd certainly think about it."

"You know what, Mariel? You think too much."

She got into the car. "Goodbye, Jake. I hope everything goes well with you," she said, in a tone that was too formal by far.

"How can it?" he said, exasperated. "You know how I feel about you."

"I wish you wouldn't try to make me feel guilty," she whispered around the lump in her throat.

"All right," he said.

He shoved his hands down in the pockets of his water-stained red-and-black jacket and stared at her intently, as if that alone would make her stay.

Mariel tried again to picture him in the city, but he looked even more rugged and rough-hewn here, amid the buildings of the town, than he had in the woods.

She concentrated on putting the key into the ignition and starting the car's engine. When she eased out of the parking space, Jake stood back. She managed a brief smile that he didn't return. He watched her until she reached the corner and turned it. She wondered how long he would stand there.

As for her, she was on her way home, to her snug apartment, her friends and her life. Soon the town of Tellurian was behind her, no more than a dot on the map spread out on the seat next to her.

She never remembered what was between Tellurian and Pittsburgh. It flew by in a blur, less real to her than the castle and the time she had spent there.

When she reached home, Jake's message was waiting on her answering machine.

"Mariel, I miss you. When you decide to come back, I'll be here."

She erased the message. Jake was out of her life. Christmas was over. The magic was gone.

Chapter Fourteen

After a lackluster New Year's Eve spent at a boring party, and an equally uninspiring New Year's Day, during which she tried in vain to find something interesting to watch on television, Mariel tried to resume her former life. She spent too many hours sitting at her word processor, elevating the act of staring at her notes on Christmas folklore to a fine art. Writing about the mistletoe shooters seemed impossible; her hastily scribbled jottings made little sense, and her actual memory of the men and boys who had come calling at the castle on Christmas night was vague.

She certainly had no trouble recalling the hours before their appearance, when she and Jake had made love so joyously in the chamber off the gallery. It was easy to picture the glow in his eyes, and the answering passion that had made her urge him closer and closer, until their bodies blended into one. She remembered every moment as if it had been distilled down to its basic elements, clear and crystalline in her memory.

One Saturday in mid-February, with an air of determination, she sat down at her keyboard and typed *The Mistletoe Shooters* at the top of her computer screen. But, as always when she thought about their interlude in the castle, she found herself adrift in visions of making love with Jake. She wondered if Jake found that happening to him, too.

Not that she would ever ask him. He had called a few times, reporting that Jessica was thriving with her foster family, but Mariel had been pointedly unresponsive. When he left messages on her answering machine, she ignored them.

It was just as well that their connection had been broken, and yet sometimes, when she sat down to her solitary dinner, or when she spotted another tall, rugged, broad-shouldered man in a crowd, she felt a sudden, sharp pain in her heart. She had never dreamed that she was capable of missing someone so much.

But she'd better stop mooning over him. Right now she was supposed to be working, not thinking about Jake.

"Mariel, are you home?" called a voice outside her front door. It was Ellie, her friend and neighbor from down the hall.

"Come in, Ellie, the door's unlocked," she called back.

She heard the latch open and close, followed by footsteps clicking smartly down the hall. In a few seconds Ellie appeared in the doorway to her office.

"I brought you a cup of coffee." Ellie deposited a foam cup from the pancake restaurant around the corner onto Mariel's desk.

"Nice," Mariel said, managing a quick smile of thanks.

"It's a bribe to make you come shopping with me," Ellie said brightly. "We can take advantage of all these President's Day sales." Ellie folded herself onto the futon across from Mariel's desk and flipped her dark hair back from her face. She waited expectantly.

Mariel shook her head. "I don't think so, Ellie. Thanks for asking, but—" She gestured helplessly at the array of papers surrounding her. "Too much work to do. You can see what a mess this is."

"Crazy you. It's the weekend, and you should get out. Are you sure you won't change your mind?"

"I appreciate the coffee. It was sweet of you. Why don't you stay for a while and visit?"

"No, if I can't convince you to come along with me, I'll be on my way. I've had my eye on a lacy teddy since Christmas, and I'm hoping it'll be marked down."

Mariel tried to show interest. "Is it that black one that opens down the front? The one we admired in the window of our favorite boutique?"

"That's it, all right. If I buy it, Leo is in for a sexy night tonight. Did I tell you that we've decided to have a baby?"

"No. No, Ellie, you didn't, but I'm happy for you," Mariel said.

Ellie lifted her eyebrows. "You don't *look* happy, sourpuss. What's the matter? Ever since you wrecked your car in that backwater section of Virginia, you've seemed...well, one step removed from what's going on around you."

"It was difficult," Mariel said.

"I know, I know. Spending Christmas in a cave and a run-down old castle sounds awful, especially since it was with some rustic who probably doesn't even speak standard English," Ellie said, "and finding a baby under such strange circumstances must have been *too* awful for words."

"Oh, but Jake wasn't—" Mariel began, but Ellie wasn't in the mood to let her finish.

"Have they found the baby's parents?"

"I don't believe so," Mariel said quietly, inspecting her fingernails.

"Odd. I can't imagine how a baby could have ended up in the woods. Well, like I said, I'd better go before all the bargains are gone." Ellie stood up and tossed her own empty cup into the wastebasket. "What are you working on that's so important?"

Mariel sighed. "I'm hoping to finish writing down some of the stories I picked up in Virginia. A university press is interested in publishing the final manuscript."

"Great. I can't wait to see what you've been up to for all these years," Ellie said. She blew Mariel a kiss before disappearing out the door.

After Ellie had gone, Mariel stared at her empty computer screen for a while. She shuffled her notes. She pulled a loose hangnail off her thumb. The phone rang, but she ignored it. It was probably Ellie again, wanting her to change her mind about going shopping. She didn't intend to, mostly because she couldn't bear to be around Ellie and her happiness these days—Ellie couldn't stop talking about her wonderful husband and her perfect marriage, and now Mariel might as well steel herself to hear Ellie run on and on about the baby she was planning to have.

A *baby*. And after Ellie gave birth and Mariel went to visit, bearing gifts, if would only remind Mariel of Jessica. And Jake, of course.

Of course. After all, what *didn't* remind her of Jake? Somehow, over the past month and a half, Mariel had managed to relate everything in her life to him. She couldn't eat without thinking about the time she had fed him the apple in the cave, when his lips had brushed her fingers. She couldn't sleep without wishing he was curled around her, his legs warming hers. She couldn't do anything, because all she could think about was Jake.

She stood up and wrapped her arms around herself, suddenly chilled. She and Jake had really had something together—and now neither of them had anything. In the face of adversity, in the space of a few short days, they had somehow managed to build a loving, caring relationship—and she had walked away from it.

She was thirty years old. In her life, she had learned that love wasn't easy to find. You couldn't manufacture it, and you couldn't buy it. Love was a gift. And, when it had been given to her, she had been unable to accept it. She must be the all-time fool, the consummate idiot.

She did what she should have done a long time ago. She marched into her bedroom and raked an armful of clothes off the rod in the closet. She pulled a suitcase from the closet shelf and chucked the clothes into it. She scooped underwear from a dresser drawer, cosmetics from the bathroom shelf. It was enough—it was all she would need for her trip to Tellurian.

Because she was going to Jake, now, today, and she wouldn't look back. There would be no more sitting down and eating a lonely dinner for one in her silent apartment. No more daydreaming at work; she'd call on Monday and request an indefinite leave of absence. No more waking up at night and thinking she heard Jessica crying.

Come to think of it, she thought she heard a baby crying even now. She lugged her suitcase into the hall and stopped to listen for a moment, because it was such a faint sound. Finally, she realized that the noise was coming from the street.

She went to the window and adjusted the blinds so that she could look down from her second-floor apartment into the parking lot. The lot was full, but she made out an unfamiliar pickup truck parked in a visitor's parking space.

Snow had begun to fall, making it hard to see what was going on. She didn't see anyone—until a man carrying a baby walked around the pickup.

The man was tall, and he was wearing a navy wool jacket over faded blue jeans and work boots. He was concentrating on the baby, jiggling it in his arms, his head bent down as if he were speaking to it in a low tone. Mariel's heart stopped beating in her chest.

It couldn't be. But it was.

Mariel flew to the door and tore it open, rushing out on the landing as Jake Travis entered the downstairs vestibule and stomped the snow off his boots. She stared at him down the open stairwell until he instinctively looked up. Jessica looked up, too, her mouth open, her eyes wide. She emitted a small hiccup.

"Jake! What—what are you doing here?" Mariel gasped, unbelievingly. Just when she had been going to go to him, *he* had come to *her*.

"I brought a visitor," he said, turning Jessica so that Mariel could see her better.

"But— How? Why?"

He grinned at her, his eyes merry. "Why not?"

"How did you get here?" Her voice was strangled in her throat.

"In my new pickup. Aren't you going to invite us in? It's cold down here."

"I'm sorry," Mariel said as Jake hurried up the stairs, the baby round-eyed with wonder in his arms. Almost afraid to look at them for fear they would vanish, Mariel led the way into her apartment.

When she turned around, she realized that Jake was taller than she remembered, and she had almost forgotten about the bicuspid that overlapped the adjoining tooth.

He glanced at the white walls of her apartment, with their carefully chosen and nicely framed art prints, at the fireplace with its brass screen, at the gleaming hardwood floors. "Nice place," he said briefly, eyeing her suitcase by the door.

"You got a new jacket," Mariel said, momentarily flustered.

"I figured the other one was past saving after I fell in a moat," he said.

"I can't get used to the way you look in this one," Mariel said.

"You'll have to," he said. He hadn't stopped smiling.

Mariel suddenly remembered her manners. "I'll hang your jacket for you," she said.

"Here, you'd better take Jessica. I can manage the jacket." And then Mariel was holding Jessica in her arms again, was pressing her hot cheek against Jessica's cool one, was inhaling the scent of her soft, sweet baby skin. Memories flooded back, memories of her happiness, and she was overcome by a sense of loss.

Jake found the hall closet and hung his coat inside. He wore a red turtleneck under a blue chambray shirt, and he looked wonderful.

"I'd bet Jessica is ready for a diaper change," he said.

"Your turn or mine?" Mariel said through a blur of tears, but she laughed with Jake.

She hadn't noticed the diaper bag when he had first come in.

"This time I have all the necessary equipment. Flubbies," he said, digging deep in the bag and producing a disposable diaper with a flourish. "Something called a puddle pad. And a pacifier. Great little gadget, a pacifier. We should have had one in that cave. It works like a plug. Sure wish they'd make one for the other end of babies. Now, that would be something."

Mariel ignored this. "Jessica has grown so much." She marveled as she laid the baby on the couch. She unzipped Jessica's warm suit and felt the little arms and legs. She couldn't believe that the child was actually lying in front of her, waiting for a diaper change.

"And she eats a lot," Jake said. "She eats cereal now, don't you Jessica?"

For an answer, Jessica blew bubbles.

"I brought a bed for her. She'd probably like a nap," Jake said after Mariel had changed the baby's diaper.

Mariel had all kinds of questions, but they had to wait until Jake went back to the pickup and brought in a portable crib, which they set up in Mariel's tiny office.

Jake spared a quick look at the papers spread over the top of her desk. "Doing lots of work, it looks like," he said.

"Let's go into the living room," Mariel said. "I need to know—I need to know all kinds of things, Jake."

She led him into the living room, conscious of him close behind her. When they sat on the couch, he said,

"I saw your suitcase in the hall. Are you going away or coming back?"

She might as well tell him she was planning to drive to Tellurian, that in fifteen minutes more she would have been on the road.

"I was—"

"Because if you're planning to go away for the weekend, you might as well forget it. I have some things to say to you, and I'm going to say them."

"I was—"

"I tried to let you know that I was coming to Pittsburgh this weekend, but you never returned my calls. Now that I'm here, you're going to hear me out, whether you like it or not."

"But I was—"

"Why didn't you call me back?"

Mariel gave up. He had no intention of listening to her—yet. So, first things first. She'd listen. She'd answer questions. And she figured that while she was at it, she might as well be honest.

"I wanted to call you more than once. But it seemed—futile. I thought it would make it all the harder to hear about Jessica and about your life and—well, I was trying to protect myself," she said, hoping he appreciated her candor.

"They haven't found Jessica's parents yet, Mariel. There are no clues, no leads. No one reported a child missing, and no one was seen in that remote area around the time that we found her," Jake said.

"How do you happen to have her?"

"I go to see her every day at her foster parents' house. Sometimes they let me baby-sit. They don't mind if I borrow her for a day or two. But they're going to have to give her up."

"Oh, that's too bad. Jessica seems so happy and well adjusted," Mariel said.

"I'm worried that Social Services won't be able to place her in a home that's nearly as good. I thought—" He stopped talking.

"What, Jake?" she asked gently.

He turned to look at her, golden flecks swimming up from the depth of those deep brown eyes.

"You're coming home with me. We're going to adopt Jessica. We're going to get married."

She felt a bubble of laughter in her throat. The timing couldn't be better. She was already packed.

"I don't want to hear all your reasons why we can't get married. We *can*," he said in a rush.

"I was already—"

"I love you. You love me. We both love the baby. You can't deny it," he said.

Deep within her, Mariel felt a wellspring of love, and hope, and joy. He loved her. She loved him. They both loved Jessica. It was all so simple, so elemental.

"Will you, Mariel? Will you marry me?" As if from a great distance, Mariel watched him reach for her hands, saw him capture them both in his, saw him lean forward and kiss her on the lips. But she didn't feel it. She didn't feel a thing.

"I—I—" she stammered, because even though she had dreamed of such a moment, her dreams hadn't prepared her for the reality of sitting across from Jake Travis and hearing him speak the words.

"I'll always love you, Mariel. When you drove away from Tellurian, I felt like my life was over. I don't want to go on without you. We're a good team. We were happy together with Jessica. So we're going to get married," he finished.

"I was already packed," she managed to say. "I was coming to see you. I was going to leave in a matter of minutes."

He stared at her, then threw his head back and laughed. "Why didn't you tell me?" he asked.

"You didn't give me a chance," she retorted.

"I've got it all planned. You can work on those Christmas legends in Tellurian in my big house, where there's a room that will make a wonderful office for you. We're going to stay in that house, Mariel. It's time to settle down. I can't wait for you to see it. There are four bedrooms, and lots of bathrooms, and a kitchen that I designed myself. And closets, lots of closets. And a large bed that's too big for me. Oh, and a nook off the master bedroom that will make a perfect nursery."

"I don't believe this is happening," Mariel said, her mind reeling. "I don't believe you're saying all these things."

"What do you want? Shall I go down on my knees to propose?"

"No, you don't have to do that," she said, but before the words were out of her mouth, Jake was on one knee in front of her.

"My lady, my love, will you do you me the honor of marrying me?"

"Oh, Jake, get up. This feels so ridiculous."

"I'm not getting up until you tell me your answer," he said firmly.

For a split second, she wondered how she could help loving this man. How could she not want to recapture the magic she had found at Christmas and hold it close to her heart all the rest of their lives?

"This might help." Jake fumbled in his pocket and pulled out a sprig of mistletoe. Mariel looked blank.

She knew what it was, of course, but what was it doing in Jake's pocket in the middle of February?

"Before I tossed my old jacket in the trash, I checked the pockets, and I found this. I kept it as a memento of Christmas, the best Christmas of my life, because I found you and Jessica," he said.

"But why did you bring it now?" she asked.

"To help us recapture the magic," he said, standing up and pulling her with him. He held the mistletoe over their heads. "How's it working?"

"Kiss me, and I'll tell you," she said, lifting her lips to his.

He did kiss her, slowly and thoroughly, but she didn't tell him anything—at least not with words—until much, much later.

Epilogue

"Where do you want to drape this garland?" Jake asked, holding up the strand of evergreen boughs and studying it critically.

"How about on the banister?"

"Let's go see how it looks," Jake said. He paused to restrain the two little hands that were reaching toward the bulbs on the Christmas tree. "No, Jessica."

"Give me a heave up," Mariel said, waving at him.

He clasped her hand and pulled. "Up you go," he said, and, once on her feet, she slid an arm around his waist. "Feeling okay?" Jake asked her.

"Wonderful," Mariel said, smiling up at him fondly.

He patted her protruding stomach. "Can't have our little mother overexerting."

"I'm only five months pregnant."

"Since we think you conceived over the Fourth of July weekend, this baby's going to be a real firecracker."

"Have you ever noticed how holidays play a big part in our love story?" Mariel asked, pressing a hand to the small of her back as Jake measured the garland against the banister.

"Yes, and if we're lucky, maybe the Easter bunny will bring the new baby right after our adoption of Jessica is final." Jake adjusted the garland. "How does this look?"

"Terrific. Leave the garland on the stairs, and I'll tie it on with big red bows. I love the way you refinished the banister, by the way. You exactly matched the shade of the stain we put on the floor."

"I had good decorating advice from my wife," he said, swinging around the newel post and planting a kiss on her lips.

"Dadadada," said Jessica, crawling over to tug at the hem of Jake's jeans, unwilling to be ignored.

Jake bent down and swung her into his arms. "Leave the red ribbon on the steps, and I'll tie the garland on myself later," he told Mariel. "I don't want to take any chances that you might trip on the stairs."

"I walk up and down the stairs every day," Mariel protested. Her new office, where she worked while Jessica napped in a crib with her name carved into the headboard in a cheery yellow-papered nursery, was at the head of the stairs, right next to the master bathroom.

"That's different. Say, isn't it time for me to see those things you've been knitting lately? Why don't you hang our stockings by the chimney with care?" he suggested.

She smiled at him and lifted her eyebrows. "In hopes that Saint Nicholas soon will be there?"

"Hey, Mariel, you don't have to convince me. Santa Claus is real. Last year I finally got a couple of Christmas presents I'd always wanted—you and this little Christmas angel," he said, nuzzling Jessica's neck.

Mariel opened a drawer in the table beside the rocking chair that Jake had lovingly refinished for her, and she took out a tissue-wrapped package.

"Have I ever told you about looking at the tapestry on the wall of the castle right before we left in the Jeep?" she asked.

"No. Did it look better up close than it did from far away?"

"I thought the tapestries were pretty," she protested.

"I was blinded by your beauty, I guess, because I didn't notice them at all."

Mariel crumpled the tissue paper and threw it at him. "Anyway," she said, moving cumbersomely toward the mantel, "I took a good look, and I saw the unicorn part, and the knights-jousting-in-the-meadow part, and there was one other part that I almost missed. It was something I've never seen in any other tapestry."

"Don't be so mysterious, Mariel. What are you trying to say?"

She kept her head turned as she affixed the biggest stocking, Jake's, to the mantel. "In the last tapestry, the one that was closest to the shadowy corner, there was a depiction of a round little man with a long white beard. He was riding in a sleigh pulled by reindeer," she said carefully.

"This was in a medieval tapestry?" Jake said skeptically.

"I don't know that it was an authentically *old* medieval tapestry, but yes, there he was, looking exactly like the man from the Magic Minimart, looking exactly like—"

"Like Santa Claus," Jake finished for her.

Mariel finished tacking her stocking to the mantel and began to hang Jessica's smaller one. "Exactly," she said.

"I've always wondered about the fact that the castle was supposed to be owned by a guy named Mr. Nicholas. And I've never heard from him, even though I left my name and address and offered to pay for the food we ate. Mariel, why are you hanging five stockings?"

"For our family," she said carefully, turning so that he could see her figure profiled against the flames in the fireplace.

"Our family consists of you, me, Jessica, and the new baby. That's four people, which equals four stockings," he said.

She slanted a sly look out of the corners of her eyes. "Don't you realize that I'm gaining more weight than most expectant mothers at five months? Don't you know what I'm trying to tell you?"

Jake stared. His gaze dropped to her abdomen, which strained against her perky maternity top.

"Twins?" he said, as if he couldn't believe it. "Are we going to have twins?"

She walked up to where he stood in the archway between foyer and living room, a mistletoe ball suspended above his head. She put her arms around him, including Jessica in their embrace. "Twins," she confirmed, leaning over her stomach to kiss him on the cheek.

"But that's . . . that's . . ."

"The very best kind of magic," she said, and she kissed him again.

HARLEQUIN®

AMERICAN ◆ ROMANCE®

Meet four of the most mysterious, magical men...in

MORE THAN MEN

In January, make a date with Gabriel...
He had a perfect body, honey-brown hair and sea-blue eyes, and when he rescued Gillian Aldair out of the crumbled mass of earth that was an Andes landslide, Gillian swore she'd never seen a man quite like him. But in her wildest imagination, she could never know just how different Gabriel was....

Join Rebecca Flanders for **#517 FOREVER ALWAYS**
January 1994

Don't miss any of the MORE THAN MEN titles!

When the only time you have for yourself is...

STOLEN moments ™

Christmas is such a busy time—with shopping, decorating, writing cards, trimming trees, wrapping gifts....

When you do have a few *stolen moments* to call your own, treat yourself to a brand-new *short* novel. Relax with one of our Stocking Stuffers— or with all six!

Each STOLEN MOMENTS title
is a complete and original contemporary romance that's the perfect length for the busy woman of the nineties! Especially at Christmas...

And they make perfect **stocking stuffers**, too! (For your mother, grandmother, daughters, friends, co-workers, neighbors, aunts, cousins—all the other women in your life!)

Look for the STOLEN MOMENTS display in December

STOCKING STUFFERS:

HIS MISTRESS Carrie Alexander
DANIEL'S DECEPTION Marie DeWitt
SNOW ANGEL Isolde Evans
THE FAMILY MAN Danielle Kelly
THE LONE WOLF Ellen Rogers
MONTANA CHRISTMAS Lynn Russell

HSM2

 **WORLDWIDE LIBRARY**

Relive the romance...
Harlequin® is proud to bring you

by Request™

A new collection of three complete novels every
month. By the most requested authors, featuring
the most requested themes.

Available in January:

WESTERN
LOVING

They're ranchers, horse trainers, cowboys...
They're willing to risk their lives.
But are they willing to risk their hearts?

Three complete novels in one special collection:

RISKY PLEASURE by JoAnn Ross
VOWS OF THE HEART by Susan Fox
BY SPECIAL REQUEST by Barbara Kaye

Available wherever Harlequin books are sold.

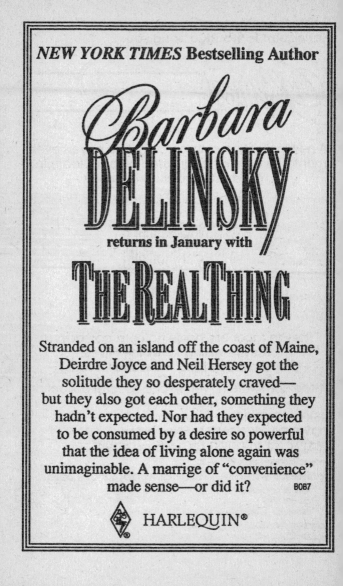

NEW YORK TIMES Bestselling Author

Barbara
DELINSKY

returns in January with

THE REAL THING

Stranded on an island off the coast of Maine,
Deirdre Joyce and Neil Hersey got the
solitude they so desperately craved—
but they also got each other, something they
hadn't expected. Nor had they expected
to be consumed by a desire so powerful
that the idea of living alone again was
unimaginable. A marrige of "convenience"
made sense—or did it?

B0B7

HARLEQUIN®

Tis the Season

...for family gatherings and holiday parties. This month's authors have put together some of their favorite recipes for Christmas dinner. Start with a *Hot Broccoli Dip.* Then serve *Standing Rib Roast* and *Copper Pennies.* Top this off with *No-Fuss, All-Sin Chocolate Truffles!*

Pamela Browning's Copper Pennies

2 lbs carrots
1 cup canned tomato soup, undiluted
1/2 cup salad oil
1 cup sugar
3/4 cup vinegar
1/2 green pepper, chopped
1 small onion, finely chopped
1 tsp prepared mustard
1 tsp Worcestershire sauce

Peel, slice and cook raw carrots until tender. Drain and cool. Combine remaining ingredients and marinate carrots in sauce in refrigerator overnight.
Can be made a few days ahead of time and keeps well in refrigerator for a week. Serves 8-10.

For the remaining three recipes, see the other December American Romances. Happy Holidays!

RECIPE4

MEN · MADE IN · AMERICA

Fifty red-blooded, white-hot, true-blue hunks
from every State in the Union!

Look for MEN MADE IN AMERICA! Written by some
of our most poplar authors, these stories feature fifty of
the strongest, sexiest men, each from a different state in
the union!

Two titles available every other month at your favorite
retail outlet.

In January, look for:

DREAM COME TRUE by Ann Major (Florida)
WAY OF THE WILLOW by Linda Shaw (Georgia)

In March, look for:

TANGLED LIES by Anne Stuart (Hawaii)
ROGUE'S VALLEY by Kathleen Creighton (Idaho)

You won't be able to resist MEN MADE IN AMERICA!